DEADLY DIALOGUE

Arden Harden, the scriptwriter, was in fine form. "Our producer is a real triple-threat man," he said.

"Yeah. He lies, he cheats and he steals."

"Does he hate McCue too?" I asked.

"He ought to, Mr. Tracy," said Harden. "Everyone ought to."

"Tami Fluff seemed to like McCue enough," I said.

"Know why they call them starlets?" Harden asked.

"No. Why?"

"Because piglets was already taken."

"You ought to think about giving up Hollywood," I said.

"You don't sound happy."

"Where else can I make a quarter of a million dollars for two weeks work?" Harden said. Then he said, "It's going to be a miracle if we get through this weekend without a murder."

"Pray for a miracle," I said.

But I didn't have a prayer. . . .

TRACE
GETTING UP WITH FLEAS

WARREN MURPHY

A SIGNET BOOK

NEW AMERICAN LIBRARY

PUBLISHER'S NOTE

NAL BOOKS ARE AVAILABLE AT QUANTITY DISCOUNTS WHEN USED TO PROMOTE PRODUCTS OR SERVICES. FOR INFORMATION PLEASE WRITE TO PREMIUM MARKETING DIVISION, NEW AMERICAN LIBRARY, 1633 BROADWAY, NEW YORK, NEW YORK 10019.

SIGNET, SIGNET CLASSIC, MENTOR, ONYX, PLUME, MERIDIAN and NAL BOOKS are published by New American Library, 1633 Broadway, New York, New York 10019

First Printing, March, 1987

1 2 3 4 5 6 7 8 9

PRINTED IN THE UNITED STATES OF AMERICA

For Billy and Karen,
Friends in deed

1

Trace's Log:

"You'd forget your head if it weren't up your ass."

The nerve of the woman, saying that to me. It called for a snappy rejoinder.

"Oh, yeah?" I said.

"Yeah. Where the hell are the title papers for the condominium?" she said.

And I said, "I don't know. I can't be expected to remember every little thing."

"Trace, you're hopeless. You could solve America's toxic-waste problem."

"Huh?" It'd been my morning for snappy rejoinders.

"The government could give you all the waste to dispose of. You'd put it somewhere and five minutes later you'd have forgotten where. No one would ever see it again. End of problem."

"This kind of rancorous attitude isn't helping us solve your problem," I said graciously.

"My problem? *My* problem? Trace, I am here in Vegas as a favor to you, subletting *your* condominium. I am willing to do everything, just as I have always done

7

everything since the first day I met you. But I can't do it without the title papers, you moron."

She kind of shrieked "moron." I think she was getting upset with me.

"Well, Chico, if they're not in the medicine cabinet, there's only two places I can think of where the papers might be."

"I'm listening."

"Either rolled up inside my sneakers in the back of the closet or hidden under the sweat suit you gave me two years ago. I think it was a Halloween gift. It's in a box in the back of the closet."

"Is there some logic to those two hiding places?" she asked.

"Yes. Two places that are out of the way and never going to be disturbed by me."

"For your sake, I hope the papers are there."

"Me too," I said.

"Did my gun permit come yet?"

"No," I said.

"What are you doing?"

"I'm getting ready to go see Groucho. He's got some kind of job for the agency."

"Good," she said. "Make money. Where's Sarge?"

"He's got a divorce case."

"Anything interesting?" she asked.

"No. Some nice, well-meaning guy wants to put aside the evil, ill-tempered Eurasian witch who has made his life a hell on earth. Just your routine case."

"Harrr," said my evil Eurasian roommate. "Are you taking care of yourself? Have you eaten yet?"

"Not yet. I was going to see Groucho and then I was going to grab some breakfast at Bogie's."

"Breakfast? It's already noon in New York."

"I don't like to hurry things," I said.

"Have you been drinking a lot?" she said.

"Hardly anything at all."

"What are you going to have for breakfast?" she asked.

"I don't know. I hadn't given it any thought."

"That means you're going to start drinking, doesn't it?"

"You are very suspicious for a woman twenty-two hundred miles away with no power to check up on me," I said. "I'm going to have eggs. Yum, yum, I want eggs."

"What kind of eggs?"

"An omelette. I'm going to have an omelette. Are you satisfied?"

"If you're not lying to me," she said.

"I never lie to you. Except about women. How long's it going to take you to do whatever it is you're doing out there?"

"A week or so. I've got to pack and show this place to people and sign papers and quit my job, and it's a real pain in the ass, Trace."

"I'm sorry, Chico."

"A week," she said.

"I count the minutes."

"Don't forget. An omelette," she said.

"I promise."

"Cross your heart and hope to die?"

"Maybe a lingering illness," I said. "Not death."

"That's good enough," she said. "Call tomorrow."

So I hung up the phone and I got out this stupid tape recorder, and here I am, killing time because I don't want to go see Groucho. Talk about a midlife crisis. Here I am, forty years old, and I'm going to be a private detective because my roommate wants to carry a gun. What government in its right mind would let someone named Michiko Mangini carry a gun?

The only thing you can be sure of about life is that it's going to get complicateder and complicateder. I used to think things were pretty good. I had a condo in Las Vegas, and I worked once in a while investigating claims for the insurance company, and Chico and I got along.

Everything's all right, see. Maybe not perfect, but when you consider my ex-wife and her kids, it's about an eight out of a possible ten.

I know how this world works, though. God waits for you to reach eight and then he gives you trouble. If you stay at seven out of ten, he leaves you alone forever. But get to eight, and it's flashing red lights and sirens all the way and people throwing rocks through your windows.

So God sees me at eight and He strikes and Chico decides she's going to leave me because I have no future and one thing leads to another, and before you know it, here I am, sitting in my father's office in New York, the worst city in the whole goddamn world except for Bombay, being an operative in my old man's private-detective agency. Chico too. She's back in Vegas now, renting out the condo and packing up all our crap, but then she's going to come out here and be a private detective and I know she's going to shoot somebody first thing because all that woman wants is power. I bet that if the Japanese were all six feet tall instead of midgets, World War II never would have happened.

Little people are sneaky. This is one of my rules. And nasty. Like Chico. She's always telling me I've got my head up my butt and I don't know anything, and this is not true. I know a lot of things. I think all the time. Just this morning I was thinking that people who think Marilyn Monroe was a tragic figure are generally the same people who think that Robert Blake is a good actor. And I was thinking that Telly Savalas isn't the kind of guy you'd trust to watch your car while you were walking around the corner, but he's perfect for doing casino commercials because they're trying to attract people just like him.

See? I think all the time, and another thing I think is that I'm never going to tell Chico her gun permit arrived. I don't want her to have it. Mine came too, and I don't want that one either. I don't want to use a gun. I don't trust guns.

You know how it is, you have a gun and one day you're getting the hell kicked out of you. Now, if you don't have a gun, you just cover your head and whimper a lot and pretty soon the guy who's beating up on you will go away, laughing. But suppose you've got a gun. Now, you're getting your head beat in, and instead of covering your head and whimpering, you start to worry. This guy's going to kill me. If he doesn't stop soon, I'm going to lose my brain because it's going to all leak out my ears. I've got to stop this. How can I stop it? I know how. And then, *boooooommmmm*. And another one bites the dust, and then he turns out to be some Unitarian bishop from Poughkeepsie, New York, and your ass goes to jail, and that's terrible because it'll be in all the papers and your ex-wife and ex-children will find out about it and they'll come to visit you and you'll have to see them.

Maybe you don't. I'll have to check visiting regulations in various prisons because you can't be too prepared in this world.

That's why I'm sitting here with this silly tape recorder, just in case somebody comes in and throws herself across my desk and shouts, "Take me, I'm yours."

I want it on tape that I said, "A hundred dollars a day plus expenses or I'm keeping it zipped."

That, my friends, is called honor, and I have a great sense of honor even if Chico doesn't believe it. Who cares what a Japanese-Sicilian believes anyway?

Chico's so beautiful I ache to see her. I hope she never finds this tape 'cause there goes my bargaining position.

Until Groucho called and said he had work for us, this was a nice morning, a nice day for thinking good constructive thoughts, and I've thought of a lot of them, all of them about how to make money. I sure as hell am not going to sit in this office for the rest of my life waiting to hit the Pick-Six. Money doesn't find you; you have to go out and find money.

I almost did a couple of times too, except . . . Well sometimes things don't work out just right.

Like that restaurant I bought into in New Jersey. That could have been my grand slam. Except the guy I expected to run it wound up not running it, and the two trapeze artists who did wind up running it couldn't direct traffic in a cemetery.

So maybe the restaurant wasn't such a good idea. But I've had others. Mark my words, someday somebody's going to come out with a product that's after-shave lotion and mouthwash combined and all the travelers in the world of the male persuasion are going to bless him and buy a thousand jillion bottles each. I hope so because I'm getting tired of using diluted after-shave for mouthwash. But everybody laughs when I mention it to them.

And what about my idea for putting signs on the front of cars, printed backward, so that people can read them in their rearview mirrors? This could have been a big novelty item, like AMBULANCE printed backward so that people can see it. And don't tell me it's stupid. It's not any more stupid than AMBULANCE printed backward. I mean, is that dumb or what? There you are, Mrs. Fahrblungit, putzing along at thirty miles an hour and suddenly bearing down on you from behind is this vehicular apparition, siren screaming, red and blue lights flashing, whoop, whoop, whoop, scream, scream, scream, and are you really going to wait until he's only ten feet away and you can read AMBULANCE backward in your rearview mirror before you pull off to the side of the road? That whole idea fits like a Ralph Nader invention, solving a problem that doesn't exist.

But the signs would have been a great novelty item except I couldn't find a backer. The only person I know with any money who would lend it to me is Chico and she won't lend it to me either.

Oh, well. I guess I have dallied enough. It's time to go see Groucho and find out what's on his alleged mind. Time to go. Devlin Tracy, boy detective, signing off . . . no richer but wiser in the ways of the world.

And I am leaving this tape recorder in the desk.

2

Think about a squirrel. You know how they are. They freeze in one place, look around, do whatever the hell it is squirrels do, then race five feet away and do it all over again.

Now you have a picture of Groucho.

Groucho is Walter Marks and he is the vice president for claims of the Garrison Fidelity Insurance Company. Back in the blessed days when my only income was what I got investigating claims for Garrison Fidelity, I guess you could call him my boss. Now he was just another client for the far-flung Tracy and Associates Detective Agency. Sounds impressive, doesn't it? Tracy and Associates. Until you find out it's a retired cop (my father), a drunk (me), and a homicidal maniac (Chico).

Groucho wasn't crazy about the change from employer to client because it meant that he could no longer fire me. The truth, though, is he couldn't fire me even when I was a claims investigator. He and I both knew that I had the job because Robert Swenson, the president of the company, is my friend and wouldn't let me be fired. Also, even if I am a little dopey, somehow I get things figured out—usually thanks to Chico—so I've saved the company a lot of money over the past few years.

Back to squirrels. That's the way Marks moved. He would sit behind his desk, look around as if he was always surprised to see you there, and then there'd be a wild flurry of activity on his desk, like shuffle papers or something. Then he'd get up and run across the room, pause, look around, and then, arms flying, he'd do it all over again.

Now, as a characteristic, this isn't so bad—I've known women who floss their teeth in restaurants—but what was wrong was that Marks never really accomplished anything. You can forgive this in a squirrel, since they don't have anything to do anyway, but I couldn't forgive it in Marks. Actually, I couldn't forgive anything in Marks.

At any rate, there I was in his office and he's running around, from here to there, stopping and sniffing the air for walnuts or something, then running someplace else. And he's talking. Yap, yap, yap, yap. And he's little, like a squirrel.

"So it's got all the potential for a disaster," he said.

"What does?"

"What we're talking about. Have you heard a word I said, Trace?"

Actually, I hadn't paid a lot of attention to what he was talking about. What I was interested in was this big stack of supermarket newspapers on his desk, you know, *The Globe* and *Midnight* and *The Enquirer* and like that. The top one that I could see had a headline that said:

NEVER WORK AGAIN. THE AMAZING, SECRET
FORMULA FOR AMASSING WEALTH WHILE YOU SLEEP.

It was one of those headlines that you're supposed to shout out loud when you read it.

"Of course I've been listening to you," I said. "It has all the potential for disaster. I remember you saying that."

"Trace, do you want coffee?"

"No."

"You look like you need coffee," he said.

"How does a person look when he needs coffee?"

"Drunk. Eyes bloodshot and rolling back in his head. Spit dribbling down the side of his mouth, dropping onto his suit. The way you look. Have some coffee," he said, then ran across the floor to his desk, picked up the phone, and told his secretary to bring in two black coffees.

I didn't think he would appreciate it if I told him to lace mine with vodka. I decided I'd drink it raw. But I wouldn't like it. He couldn't make me like it.

We waited for his secretary and I had a chance to reflect on the fact that Walter Marks was the singular most uninteresting human being I had ever met. I could not remember his ever saying one thing that was even mildly informative, entertaining, or interesting. His clothes were dull, always three-piece navy-blue suits, and his shoes were shined, thick-soled, and practical. Even his haircut was uninteresting, smooth and neatly polished and not a hair out of place, and his fingers were always clean and his fly was always zipped. He always had socks on. He never had a flask in one of his pockets. He had average skin and some average-color eyes that I don't really recall, and the only thing unusual about him what was that he was short, real short. Minute might be the right word.

His secretary brought in the coffee. Half of it was spilled in the saucers. He sipped his and I asked him, "Why are you reading all these newspapers?"

"That's what I've been telling you. All our trouble's in there."

"I don't know. I think 'Never work again. The amazing, secret formula for amassing wealth while you sleep' isn't such a bad idea."

He looked confused. He often did that. No movement, just a puzzled look in his eyes. He set down his coffeecup and grabbed the top paper off the pile.

"That's not the story we're interested in. This is the one." He rapped on the front page of the paper a half-dozen times in quick succession: rap, rap, rap, rap, rap, rap. I was getting a headache. I wondered if squirrels had any natural predators. Owls, I guessed, and eagles, and I wished I was an owl or an eagle.

He stopped rapping and moved his finger so I could see the front page of the paper.

There was a picture of this movie actor, Tony McCue, on the front page. He had a look on his face that I had seen many times before, usually when shaving, the look of a man who is totally shitfaced from the booze.

The headline under the picture read:

TONY McCUE PLAYS WILLIAM TELL
Hollywood Hero has Stuntman Shoot Apples from Head

I leaned over to look at the paper, but Groucho said, "You don't have to read the story. The headline tells it all." He grabbed another paper. "And look at this one: 'Tony McCue dives off hotel balcony into pool.' And this one: 'Actor tries to slide down mountain on cafeteria tray.' "

He flipped through some pages. "It says the dumb bastard wants to start the Anthony McCue Downhill Slide Memorial Competition. Here's another one. 'That girl at McCue's side is his psychiatrist.' He travels with a shrink, for God's sake. Listen. 'Tony McCue beaten up in redneck bar. Slugs drunk with champagne bottle.' "

Groucho dropped the papers, put his head into his hands, and looked down. He didn't have a bald spot and I thought that was nice because a bald spot would have ruined the perfect dull symmetry of Walter Marks.

"Why me, God?" he said.

I fished around in the stack of papers.

"Here's a good one," I said. " 'Tony McCue drinks bottle of booze at bottom of hotel pool.' "

"This man is a menace," Marks said.

"I don't know. He sounds like my kind of guy."

"Wonderful," Marks said. He looked up and smiled. "Just what I wanted to hear."

"What?" I've learned always to be suspicious when Groucho says something is wonderful. That usually means it's good for him and awful for me, and I wasn't put on earth to make things good for him and if God wanted things awful for me, he would have made me Iranian.

"I said wonderful," he explained. "You like him so much, he's yours."

"You'd better explain this to me," I said. "Slowly."

"Drink your coffee," he said. "Tony McCue is ready to begin filming a movie in upstate New York. Some kind of mystery. What we have done is to write a six-million-dollar insurance policy on his life with the producers as beneficiaries. The movie will take two months to shoot and we have to keep him alive for two months. That's your job."

"Not a chance."

"Why not?"

"Because I was in upstate New York once. I came down with pneumonia and I got bitten by a catfish. I'm not spending two months there, not for you, not for Garrison Fidelity, not for Tony McCue, not for a Hollywood producer, not for the history of cinema as we know it in our lifetime."

"You're jumping to conclusions, Trace," he said.

"It's how I get my exercise. That way and moving

quickly out of the path of people, like you, who wish me ill."

"I have never met a person who takes the offer of a paid job as such a personal affront," Groucho said.

"Don't deny that you hate me and want me dead," I said.

"Have you ever thought of getting professional help, Trace? You're a paranoid."

"Just because I'm a paranoid doesn't mean that you're *not* trying to have me killed."

"Look. Try to concentrate. Drink your coffee. I am not trying to have you killed. I want you to go to this town . . ." He looked at a sheet of paper on his desk, "Canestoga Falls. I want you to hang out for ten days, two weeks. See what's going on. See what kind of shape this lunatic McCue is in. Keep him alive. Don't let him kill himself. If he's okay, you come back. If he's real nuts and self-destructive, you let me know and I'll make arrangements to send other people up there to watch him."

"You have zookeepers on your payroll?" I asked.

"No. But I can hire them somewhere, and a hell of a lot cheaper than I can hire you for."

"I don't have to stay up there for the whole two months?" I said.

"No."

"I want four hundred a day plus expenses."

"Fine," Marks said.

"Fine? You say fine? You've bitched and complained and cheated me out of every legitimate cent I ever spent on expenses and now you're telling me, just like that, fine, for four hundred dollars a day, fine? You're saying that?"

"Yes."

"You're up to something. Why pay me four hundred

dollars a day when you can hire keepers for less than that?"

"Because, while you don't know it—and, of course, being a paranoid schizophrenic with a drinking problem, you would not believe it—I have great respect for you, Trace."

"You're right, I don't believe it."

"Well, I do. I find you an insufferable waste of flesh and blood as a human being, but you have a certain native cunning in matters like this that would enable you to see dangers and pitfalls that might elude a normal person," he said.

"See? And here you thought it was never any good being a paranoid. Of course, I see dangers and pitfalls. The world is filled with them. How about the men's room at O'Hare Airport?"

"I suppose in some way that's logical to you," Marks said. He got up and ran across the room. He stopped, smelled the air, waved his arms around, and pulled some papers from on top of a file cabinet. I wished I had a BB gun.

"How'd you get involved in a deal like this?" I asked. "Insuring this lunatic?"

"Big premium, little risk." He sounded dejected as he added, "I thought."

"Then you found out exactly what you were insuring," I said.

"That's right."

"You should have canceled the policy," I said. "You do it with widows and orphans all the time."

"Mr. Swenson refused to do that," Marks said.

Swenson, as I said, was the president of Garrison Fidelity and a sometime friend of mine. If I ever thought that *I* made Walter Marks crazy, Robert Swenson sent him over the edge because he ran the insurance company on wish and whimsy with a large dollop of hangover mixed in. I think his last coup in the industry was pioneering life insurance for heavy smokers.

A lot of things suddenly came clear.

"So you're only doing this because Bob Swenson told you to?" I said.

"That's right. But I'm prepared to stand by the decision as mine," he said.

"Very noble. And I gather that's why you've offered me this job too. Because Swenson ordered you to."

"Ordered is a strong word. He suggested that you might have a certain special ability in dealing with people like Tony McCue."

"It's a compliment," I said. "Repeat it to me. I love to hear compliments from your lips."

"Actually, he said, 'Set a drunk to catch a drunk.' "

"I'll ignore that because I don't believe it," I said. "And that's why you didn't argue about my fee. He told you to pay me whatever I want."

I had him, and he didn't answer. Instead, he turned his back and pretended to be looking through the file cabinet.

"In that case, I want five hundred a day. Plus expenses."

He turned and shouted. "That's robbery."

"It's business, Groucho. I'm a very busy partner in a fast-growing private detective agency. It's going to be tough to fit you into our work schedule as it is."

He surrendered faster than I'd ever seen him surrender. "All right," he shouted. "All right. Five hundred a day. And don't call me Groucho."

"Plus expenses."

He spun around. "And you itemize those expenses. Itemize every penny of them or you don't get them. We're not running a charity ward here or some big petty-cash fund that you can dip into anytime you want. You have to itemize, do you hear me?"

"I hear you. I'll itemize. I promise. Every penny. Every parking receipt. Everything, Walter, everything." I nodded earnestly. It's good sometimes to let people save face, even if it was a face like Groucho's. My father always told me that. He said, Give the guy a graceful way to surrender. It's like if you're in a saloon fight and the other guy is down; you don't want to stand over him shouting at him because, as sure as God made insurance swindlers, the guy's going to get up and hit you with a chair. Instead, you help him up and let him know how sorry you are and it was a lucky punch and you feel terrible and the next time it would have been a far different story and you feared for your life in front of his mighty wrath and like that, and so the guy walks away feeling better and he doesn't try to get lucky with a chair.

"I won't expect a penny for any expenses I don't itemize," I said.

He nodded and I walked toward the door. "I can see myself out if you're finished, Walter."

"I wish you would. My secretary has all the data at her desk in an envelope."

"One question, though," I said.

Groucho ran back to his desk, stopped, wiggled his cheeks, and sat down.

"Yes."

"Why is Bob Swenson taking a personal interest in insuring this McCue nut?"

"I don't think his reasons are any business of yours. Or mine."

"Okay, fine," I said. That meant he didn't know why Swenson wanted to insure the star of some movie against cutting his own wrists and using his arteries to hang himself. Groucho was one of those people who, if he knew something, couldn't resist showing off that he knew it.

I picked up the envelope from his coffee-spilling secretary and stopped at Swenson's office before I left the building.

"Hello, Moneypenny," I said to his secretary. "Is S in?"

The secretary was this tall, very extravagant, very competent thirtyish blonde who had been with Swenson for six years and whom he was banging even though he had never told me that.

"No," she said. "He's in Toronto."

I hesitated a moment, waiting I guess for her to invite me for lunch or something or at least to the leather sofa in Swenson's office, but she didn't.

I didn't mind. Someday she was going to see the first wrinkle alongside her eyes and realize that she was spending the best years of her life on a married man, and then she'd look for me.

And I'd have to tell her, Not a chance, lady. Because while she was pretty good-looking, too bad, there was only one Chico in the world, and Chico made her look like goldfish food.

"Too bad," I said. "I wanted to talk to him about Tony McCue."

"The actor?"

"Yes. Gone Fishing's got a policy on him. I'm supposed to keep him alive."

"Get his autograph for me, will you?" she said.

"Sure," I said, and left. I crossed her off my list. I didn't want anything to do with women who collected autographs.

3

The only thing wrong with Bogie's Restaurant, aside from the fact that it's right downstairs from Sarge's office and much too convenient, is the people who hang out there.

They've got one whole wall covered with pictures of mystery writers who frequent the place—and if that's not enough to make you water your lawn, they've got private eyes who hang out there too.

You've got to listen to them sometimes talking to each other. It's enough to make you think there were two more Marx Brothers, Dope-o and Jerk-o. They're bad enough, and they're not all. Now, Bogie's is getting out-of-town trade too. Only about a week before, there was this private detective from Boston who stopped in. He had a quiche cookbook under one arm and he ordered some kind of Yugoslavian beer and got drunk after two sips and then wanted to talk to the bartender about the meaning of courage.

See? Drinking in New York can be a risky business, but if you're careful and if you go to Bogie's at selected hours, you miss the private eyes and the stupid writers and then it's the best restaurant and saloon in New York City, even if the owners are always complaining that I drink too much for my own health.

Coming back from Groucho's, I looked through the front window, but I didn't see anybody who might want to talk to me so I went inside and took my usual seat in the corner of the bar near the jukebox.

Billy, the owner, was tending bar while his wife, Karen, was trying to fix the tape deck.

"The usual?" Billy said.

Shakespeare was right: conscience does make cowards of us all. I remembered what I told Chico, promising her that I would have eggs.

"Hey, you awake yet? The usual?" Billy repeated.

The usual is Finlandia on the rocks. I won't drink Russian Vodka and I can't stand American, and what do the Canadians know about vodka anyway? Besides, I figured it's only fair to drink vodka from Finland because I won't eat their Swiss cheese. I mean, if their cheese was any good, wouldn't they call it Finland cheese instead of Swiss cheese? I buy only Swiss cheese and Finnish vodka. This helps to bring order to a confusing world.

"No," I told Billy. "Not the usual."

"What, then?"

"An omelette. A vodka omelette. Hold the egg."

"Sure," he said as if it were suddenly the drink of choice in New York. His wife, Karen, is a shrink, and I thought maybe they've had orders like this before.

He poured vodka over rocks and put it in front of me, and I said, "When you see Chico, you be sure to tell her I had an omelette."

"Naturally. What else?" he said, and then he walked away and let me drink in peace, which I did until I saw

Sarge walking through our office entrance door and I went upstairs to meet him and tell him that Walter Marks was going to make our company rich for the next couple of weeks.

4

My father's name is Patrick Tracy but everybody calls him Sarge because that's what he was before he retired from the New York City police department. He's almost seventy years old and maybe two inches shorter than me, but he's still over six feet tall and he's wider than me, and if you are ever thinking of messing with the man, first look at his hands. Sarge has hands . . . Well, if you cut two thick slabs out of a six-by-six beam, those would be his palms. His fingers look like those hot smoked sausages they sell in plastic packs in the supermarket.

Anyway, when I got upstairs, Sarge was sitting behind the desk, looking through the mail, and if faces were weather forecasts, his was cloudy with a chance of rain.

He scowled at me when I walked in, and I said, "Should I come back next week when you get a chance to cool off?"

"No, come on in."

"Why are you looking like hell hath no fury like an ex-cop scorned?" I asked.

"Goddamn divorce case," Sarge said. "Nothing ever goes right."

"Tough one?"

"Tough, my ass. It's a snap. It's so damned easy that it's created a moral dilemma for me."

"It's what us big private eyes do best," I said. "Didn't you ever read Spenser?"

"To hell with Spenser. You want a beer?"

"No, I'm into eggs today."

"That's all right. I don't mind drinking alone." Sarge stood up and walked around the desk. You could tell fall was upon us because he had finally put away his gray plaid sports jacket and taken his dark-blue suit out of the closet. He went into the small bathroom where he keeps bottles of beer in the back of the toilet-tank. This is a habit I find totally disgusting, but when I called him on it, Sarge told me it was because I didn't understand plumbing and the water that goes into the back of the toilet tank was clean. I said if it was so clean, how come the inside of the tank is brown and has hair on it? Slimy hair.

He said it was my imagination. I offered him a glass of water from the toilet tank as a toast to my imagination. He poured it down the sink and suggested that I had become a quiche-eater in my later years.

He's probably right. Anyway, Sarge got a beer from the back of the toilet tank, twisted the bottle cap off as if it had been personally responsible for the kind of day it had been, and took a long swallow before going back around to his desk.

"Oh, the divorce. Right. I told you, this guy hires us to check on his wife 'cause he thinks she's tipping on him. So I'm stashed outside the house this morning and he goes to work, eight o'clock on the stroke. I'm ready for the long haul. I figure we can drag this one out for weeks, hundred and fifty a day plus, and we'll knock them dead and make Chico happy when she comes back because we're finally making some money."

"Good plan," I said. "What went wrong?"

"The husband leaves at eight o'clock. Eight-o-five, this florist delivery truck rolls up and this guy gets out who's got muscles, twenty-five years old, rolled up T-shirt, tight-ass jeans, no socks. God, I hate people who don't wear socks."

"Very big in California," I said.

"I know. I guess that's why I hate it so much. Anyway, this guy gets out of the truck and walks up to the house. He bips the bell and the door opens like a flash of light. I figure he must have been parked down the block waiting for the husband to leave and then zipped up to the house. So now I got him inside with the wife, and I don't know who the guy is or what's going on, so I figure I'd better reconnoiter the house a little bit. First I wait five minutes or so, just to see if maybe he really came to take an order for flowers or something or ask directions, but when he doesn't come out, I figure it's time."

"So far, so good," I said. "Just the way they teach it at Famous Detectives' School."

"So I go down alongside the house, between the house and some high hedges, heading for the back yard. Nobody can see me because the hedges are so high, so I'm safe, and I stop alongside the windows to listen if I can hear anything."

"Squealing? Oohs and ahhs?" I said.

"Right. But there isn't any, so I get to the gate leading to the back yard and I'm wondering about going in, or maybe I should go up and ring the doorbell and ask for directions, and if the woman doesn't answer or if she's in a bathrobe, then I know I've got her."

"Why didn't you do it? It sounds smart to me," I said.

"I was going to. Then I heard a sound."

"A squeal? An oooh or an ahhh?"

"More like a little grunt, from the back yard. So I go up to the gate, and would you believe it, there's the two of them on a picnic table in the back yard and he's porking her, right there on the picnic table, right out in God's good golden sunshine."

"Sounds real romantic. What'd you do?"

"Don't you want to know what she looked like?" he asked me. "It makes a better story."

"Sarge, what did she look like?"

"She was beautiful, son. Long red hair and a wonderful body and just beautiful."

"What'd you do then?"

"I used my handy-dandy little camera and I sneaked a dozen pictures of them flagranting the delicto and then I got out of there."

"The guy didn't spot you? You didn't get punched in the face or arrested or something?"

"Hey. I said the guy was big. I didn't say he was that big," Sarge said.

"After you left, you lost the camera?" I said.

"No."

"The film was exposed to the light."

"No," he said.

"I don't understand then what's making you look like a commercial for Alka-Seltzer."

"Because I'm on the job for fifteen minutes and it's done. A hundred and a half a day for a divorce and I wind up with some round-heeled bimbo who's screwing the first guy she sees. I thought we had at least a week's work out of this job." He finished the beer with one gargantuan pull on the bottle that made it seem like he was going to suck the color off the inside of the brown glass.

"And now I'm stuck," he said. "I don't want to be

lying to a client, telling him I didn't find out anything when I already did. All the private eyes I used to run into on the job would do that, just keep their meter running as long as they could, and I hate that 'cause it's cheating. I don't want to do it. But I don't think it's fair either that I've got this case nailed down inside a half-hour. See? I told you. A moral dilemma."

"No big deal," I said.

He didn't hear me. He said, "Why couldn't I draw an ex-nun who's got to be wooed and wined and seduced slowly, not somebody who's getting pronged by some delivery boy right in the middle of the back yard?"

"Maybe it was rape," I said hopefully. "Rape doesn't count. You'd have to give her credit for a rape."

"I thought of that. Until she started cooperating in other ways. I remember that old joke. Feel sorry for her, her mother went down on the *Titanic*. This was the mother."

"As I said, it's no big deal. You're making a mistake in logic. You're forgetting that one swallow does not a summer make."

"I saw her swallow too," Sarge said. "And I've got it on film."

"But it's not enough. You give just this much to the husband and you're going to find out in divorce court that the woman was on medication today that affected her judgment, or she met this delivery boy who was her long-ago first boyfriend, the one who first plucked this innocent flower, and in a moment of madness, she succumbed to him again and it's a terrible thing that she did and she'll regret it for the entire rest of her life and she doesn't want to be divorced from her husband, the only man she ever really loved. She knows that now, even if she didn't know it when she was playing Holland Tunnel for the muscle-bound zinnia salesman. It could go on like that in court."

"What are you getting at?" Sarge said.

"Just this. You've got to make sure. You got a picture of the flower truck's license plate?"

"Of course. I'm not stupid."

"Fine. You've got to find out who he is. Where he's from. Has he got a rape record? Then you've got to find out if this is just an isolated incident or if she's putting out for everybody within ten miles of the World Trade Center. No isolated incidents allowed. I think you've got to park yourself outside that house and track the traffic. I think you've got to see if other people come, or if Flowers comes again."

"He came once. I saw him."

"Once is not enough," I said. Sarge looked doubtful and I said, "Sarge, you sent me to Jesuit college. Don't you think I know something about mental reservations?"

"About lying too," he said. "All right. I'll give it a couple more mornings, but then that's it. I won't run the fee up on our client, no matter how much we need it."

"We don't need it anymore," I said. "I'm making us rich."

"You've stopped drinking," Sarge said.

"Please. One Chico Mangini in the firm is enough. I've got us a big job from the insurance company." I told him what it was about and he said, "Five hundred dollars a day for nursemaiding a drunk? Sounds like work you were born for, boy. How long do you think it'll run?"

"I figure I might squeeze a couple of weeks out of it anyway," I said. "Just until Chico gets back here."

"When are you leaving?"

"Tomorrow morning."

"This arrived just in time, then." He held up the piece of paper. "Your gun permit."

"Yeah. Chico's came too. You didn't tell her about it, did you?"

He shook his head. "I haven't talked to her."

"Good. Don't tell her about it. She's just going to shoot somebody."

He stood up and said, "Beats getting shot." He walked to the file cabinet in the corner of the room and took out a package wrapped in newsprint.

"Here. This is for you."

He handed me the package. It weighed a ton. When I opened it on the desk, I found inside a well-oiled .38-caliber Police Special.

"Careful. It's loaded," he said.

"I don't know what to say," I said honestly.

"It was my first gun when I joined the force. I want you to have it, now that it's legal for you."

"That's wonderful, Sarge. I'll always treasure it."

A little later, he got ready to go home. Home, for him, is Middle Village, Queens. Home, for him, is my mother. Fortunately, that's his problem, not mine.

I had taken two tissues out of the box on his desk and was dusting off my shoes, a job I do once every six months whether they need it or not.

"Want to come home for dinner tonight?" Sarge said.

"No. Jesus Christ, where did you get these tissues?"

"Your mother bought them. What's wrong?"

"Where'd she get them, Tissue City? They feel like they're made out of crushed Uneeda biscuits."

"Waste not, want not, as your mother says."

"And says and says and says," I said. "Give her my love. I'll pass on dinner."

"I wish I could," he said, and when he left, he made me promise to call him from upstate as soon as I had the job figured out.

I waited until I heard the downstairs door slam shut

before I unloaded the gun and put the bullets in the desk drawer.

Then I put Chico's gun permit and the pistol under one of the couch cushions.

First of all, I wasn't going to carry a gun.

Second of all, if I did carry a gun, it wasn't going to be this relic from the O.K. Corral.

Third, if I ever did decide to carry it, I'd have to hire someone to carry it for me because it weighed forty pounds.

Fourth, I was on my way to upstate New York to make sure some drunk didn't wind up killing himself for no good reason. Who'd need a gun?

The permit and gun would be safe under the cushion because Sarge and I would never disturb them by cleaning. Chico might but only when she was convinced that Sarge and I didn't expect her to clean.

Later I realized I hadn't eaten all day and I went down to Bogie's for a sandwich. Fortunately there weren't any private detectives or writers there, so I didn't miss carrying Sarge's elephant gun. Later I took a shower in Billy and Karen's back apartment.

Then I went upstairs again and slept on the couch. I was supposed to be looking for an apartment, but I thought I'd leave that job for Chico when she arrived.

Sarge didn't know I was staying here. He thought I was staying with friends. He should have known that that wasn't very likely. I don't have any friends.

I spent the shank of the evening lying on the crusty old coach, trying not to be impaled on Sarge's elephant bazooka and reading the files Groucho gave me on Tony McCue.

McCue was born in the Midwest and had been the star of a couple of mediocre television series. He was making large amounts of money, and then, to the consternation of the business, he had packed it all in and gone to England. He was, he had said, a fraud who couldn't act as well as Lassie, and he was going to England to learn his trade. He stayed overseas for seven years, doing stagework, avoiding cameras, minding his business, and letting his name generally be forgotten. When he returned to Hollywood, he returned with a roar, starring in four hit movies in succession and quickly moving to that top rank of stars whose presence in a film could make it a hit. He had been on top now for a dozen years, and reading the newspaper clippings about him, I decided Groucho had a reason to be worried about the insurance company's investment.

I don't want anybody to think that I just generally believe everything I read in supermarket newspapers. For instance, I don't think that Michael Jackson is the marooned commander of a wrecked alien spaceship, waiting on earth for a rescue craft to come. At least, I don't believe all of it.

But I do believe that where there's a lot of smoke, there's usually at least a little fire, and all these stories made McCue out to be a nut case. He went from fistfight to lawsuit to paternity battle. He fought with directors, producers, and costars. One day he gave his stuntman the day off and spent the whole day doing dangerous stunts on a rope hanging down the side of a mountain, until the producer found out and got him down. Then the producer fired the stuntman for dereliction of duty. This prompted McCue to walk off the picture until the stuntman was rehired. That scored him one point in my book.

He had had a small heart attack. He traveled with a psychiatrist in tow. He made commercials in favor of the Vietnam War and said that Jane Fonda had cottage cheese for brains.

Two points for McCue.

He had an opinion about everything and didn't seem afraid to voice it. About one president of the screen actors' union, he said, "That man is so dumb he thinks Nicaragua is in Southeast Asia." He offered a personal reward of $50,000 for "anyone who will bring me the empty head of the Ayatollah Khomeini."

I read about all his fights and all his antics and convinced myself that Walter Marks had conned me again. Tony McCue sounded like a five-thousand-dollar-a-day job, not five hundred.

I put the file away and decided to go to sleep. I don't always sleep in my clothes, no matter what kind of lies Chico spreads about me, but I figured there wasn't much reason to take them off because I was driving upstate the next day and my clothes were going to get all wrinkled anyway from driving, so what difference did it make if they were wrinkled to start with?

Sometimes I take a lot of time thinking about things like this, and Chico will say stuff like, "All the time you've spent allegedly thinking, you could have taken your clothes off ten times by now." See? She's a woman and she thinks that just because you can do a thing quickly, maybe you ought to do it. I worry more about the rights and wrongs of things.

I quoted Strindberg at her. "Women, being small and foolish and therefore evil, should be suppressed, like barbarians and thieves."

She did not think this funny and told me that Strindberg was exceeded in stupidness only by me. I said that I didn't think a lot of truly stupid people quoted Strindberg in the first place. She said that lately there was a lot of it going around.

The telephone rang just as I closed my eyes.

"Is this Devlin Tracy?" a caller asked.

"Yes."

"This is Tony McCue. Do you know who I am?"

"Yes," I said.

"Why are you trying to make my life miserable?"

"I didn't know that I was," I said.

"Trust me. You are."

"I don't trust anybody who says 'trust me.' What do you want?"

"I want you to meet me right now."

"You're not my problem until tomorrow," I said.

"It's one minute after midnight. I'm now your problem. Somebody just told me that I couldn't walk down the white line in the middle of Fifty-seventh Street for two blocks without getting hit by a car. What do you think?"

"I think you should wait until I get there," I said.

"I thought you'd see it my way," he said.

I caught a cab about three minutes before I would have frozen to death. There are two kinds of cabdrivers in New York: one kind knows every street in the city and tells you all about it; the other kind doesn't speak any English and couldn't get you to Central Park if you started out at the Plaza Hotel across the street. This was one of the first kind, but I tuned him out as he took me uptown to where McCue was in one of those Fifty-seventh Street places, overpriced, overpublicized, overyuppied.

There was a big white Rolls-Royce parked in front of the restaurant, smack dab alongside a fire hydrant. Naturally it was unticketed. Rollses don't get ticketed in New York. After all, they might belong to a pimp or somebody important.

The restaurant that took up the back of the building was closed, but there were about a dozen people in the bar, clustered around a small table in the center of the floor. I sidled my way through the press and found

McCue sitting at a table, across from some guy who looked like Hulk Hogan, preparing to arm-wrestle him.

"All right," McCue said. "For the hat and coat."

"Okay," the other man said. Somebody was acting as referee and he'd been watching too much arm-wrestling on television because he took forever to inspect their grips and make sure everything was fair. Finally, he released their hands and said, "Go!"

If there had been an echo, it wouldn't have died out before McCue's hand was flat down on the tabletop.

The big guy jumped to his feet and yelled "Hooray." He immediately walked over to a coat rack and took down a long white suede coat and a matching white suede fedora in the Humphrey Bogart style. My guess was that the hat cost more than my whole wardrobe; the coat would have covered my net worth.

McCue got to his feet. "I guess I've got to work out more," he said. "Now that I've lost all my money and most of my clothing, somebody'll have to buy me a drink."

I stepped forward and said, "I'm Tracy. I knew you were going to be a deadbeat."

"I'll pay you back," he said. He shook my hand. He had a good strong handshake, the kind that seemed to go with a good strong face. You'd have to live on another planet not to recognize him, because his face was everywhere. McCue had made a career out of playing average-guy heroes, and the face was perfectly designed for that: wide-set, intelligent eyes, a straight nose, strong chin, and stubborn mouth.

"You do drink, don't you?" he said.

"Some claim it's what I do best."

"Good. Let's go sit over there. At least you're not some damned tee-totaler. I never had a keeper before, at least he doesn't have to be some bluenose bastard."

We sat down at the bar and I said, "One thing. Why'd you call me?"

"I had dinner here tonight with the two producers of this goddamn film I'm working on and they told me about the insurance policy. I guess they got your name from the insurance company. Anyway, after they left, I stayed and drank and started to resent you, so I found the agency number in the phone book and I figured you might as well start earning your keep because I needed you. Do you know I lost four hundred dollars arm-wrestling with that gorilla and then I lost my hat and coat? You arrived just before I promised him my first-born. He beat me fifteen times in a row."

"Shouldn't the first five losses have given you a clue to stop?" I said.

"I thought my better conditioning would tell in the end."

The bartender made us drinks: vodka on the rocks for me—because I didn't think he'd bring me a vodka omelette, hold the egg—and for McCue, he packed a glass filled to the brim with ice, then poured in straight gin until the liquid was level with the rim of the glass.

"When are you going upstate?" I asked him.

"Tomorrow. You want to drive up together?"

"No," I said. "We don't know each other well enough yet. It's one thing to meet some guy in a bar, 'cause you can always leave, but in a car for eight hours, that could be a trap with no escape. I went cross-country with my wife once and that was the end of our marriage. And it was only our honeymoon. We'd better meet up there."

"That makes sense," he said agreeably.

The big guy, now wearing the white hat and coat that used to belong to McCue, came over and handed McCue a ring of car keys.

"These were in the pocket," he said.

"Thanks, you cheat," McCue said.

The man seemed real sincere. "No, no," he said. "No cheating."

"Of course you cheated. You're stronger than me," McCue said with a grin. "I hope it rains mud on you."

The man grinned back, they shook hands, and the man left.

We had another drink and I finally said, "I've got to get some sleep. Can you drive?"

"Naturally. Did you ever know a drinker who wasn't a better driver drunk than sober?"

"Yes," I said.

"Who?"

"All of them," I said.

McCue cadged twenty dollars from me for a tip for the bartender and left with a lot of promises to come back. He was wobbling a little as we walked to the Rolls-Royce.

He offered to drive me home.

"I'm not sure yet that you can drive," I said.

"Neither am I. So driving you home will be good practice before I fool around with something valuable like my own life."

As we got into the car, a police car came whooping down the block past us.

McCue fumbled with the keys for a while, got the car started, and headed west on Fifty-seventh Street. He seemed to drive all right. Up ahead, there were a lot of flashing lights in the street.

"Something's going on," he said.

"Seems that way."

"I love police shit. Let's see what it is."

Instead of turning south and getting the hell away, like I would have done, he pulled into the block with all the police vehicles. He was finally waved down by a cop who motioned him to make a U-turn. McCue grudgingly obliged and then stopped and said, "Why don't you see what's going on?"

"Oh, bullshit. I don't care what's going on."

"Well, then, I will," he said.

Just what I needed. McCue getting arrested for drunken driving with me in the car. Groucho would not be happy. Good-bye, five hundred dollars a day.

"Stay where you are," I said. "I'll go see."

I walked down the block to where a cluster of people seemed to be standing around a white glob in the street. As I got close, I recognized the white glob. It was the body of a man wearing a white coat. A white hat lay ten feet away from the body. McCue's hat and coat.

About a block farther down Fifty-seventh Street, there were more cops and I could see now that there had been a collision between a car and a cab. An ambulance was parked down there.

I turned to walk back to the car when I heard a voice yell, "Hey. You. Wait a minute."

I turned around to look into the rock-hard face of Detective Edward Razoni. He was a New York City cop that I had bumped into on another matter. He was a madman, ill-tempered, and to make him even more perfect, he hated me.

"Tracy, right?"

"That's right. What happened?"

He waved an arm at the white lump on the ground. "Why is it that everytime we find a body, you're somewhere around? Why do you do this to me?"

His voice was as hard as his face.

"God sent me to you," I said.

"A more suspicious man than me might think you were a killer."

"It's not my ex-wife, is it?" I said.

"No, it's a man."

"Then I didn't kill him," I said. "What happened?"

"We know you didn't kill him. That car down there did." He waved toward the accident. "Ran him down and then beat it and plowed into a cab. What are you doing here anyway?"

"Just out for a pleasant evening on the town."

"Well, why don't you get out of here? You make me sick."

His partner, a big black guy named Tough Jackson, came up. He has some sense anyway. "Hello, Tracy. What are you doing here?"

I was kind of pleased that he remembered me. It's nice to be remembered by somebody besides bartenders and other degenerates.

"Just driving around, saw the lights."

"Hit-and-run. Nothing to it. Unless you know the guy."

"Yeah, take a look," Razoni said. He walked me over to where the body lay with its head split open. Still I could recognize the face. It was the big guy who had arm-wrestled McCue.

I shook my head. "Never saw him before," I said. "Guess I'd better be on my way. See you."

"Don't make it too soon," Razoni said.

I got into the passenger seat of the Rolls and McCue peeled off with a screech of rubber. With a gang of cops standing around. The silly bastard was suicidal.

"So what was it?" he said as he raced toward the corner.

"Accident. A pedestrian got hit."

"That's all?" he said, looking at me.

I said, "Watch the road, please, and head downtown. You knew the dead guy."

"Who?" he said. He looked at me again.

"The guy from the bar who won your hat and coat. He's dead."

"Hit by a car?"

"Yes."

"I bet the coat is ruined," he said.

"Unless tire tracks come in as a design," I said.

"It looked like you know the cops," he said.

"I did."

"Did you tell them who the guy was?"

"No. And I didn't mention you."

"Why not?"

"I would be very happy if your name doesn't get in the papers for the next two weeks," I said. "Besides, it was just your hat and coat. You don't know anything about it."

"It was a good coat," he said.

"Tire tracks on it," I said.

He drove downtown in silence. When he let me out in front of Bogie's, which was closed for the night, he said, "You could at least have picked up the hat. That was a good hat."

5

In the morning while I was waiting for the kid to bring the rental car around—I had asked for something nice in blue—I telephoned Chico and woke her up. I like doing this, but since I'm not up early very often, I don't get much chance. I try, though, 'cause if I get to her before she has her usual triple breakfast, she's weak from hunger and she can't argue with me too well.

I told her where I was going and what the job was and how I had met Tony McCue the night before, and she seemed to consider it awhile before answering. I knew she was thinking about food.

"What's McCue like?" she said finally.

"I don't know. I saw him lose at arm-wrestling, I saw him worry about losing a good hat, and I saw him drink. I think he puts his pants on one leg at a time."

"Come on, Trace. He's a legend in our time. You have to do better than that."

"All right. He's very handsome. Is that what you wanted to hear?"

"You're getting closer. Anything else?" she asked.

"No. Wait until I start nursemaiding him. Then I'll give you all the dirt," I said.

"Okay," she said. "Now, when you get up there, I want you to stay away from all those Hollywood chippies."

"Why?"

"Because they all got AIDS from Rock Hudson," she said.

"It's okay, Chico. The only woman in Hollywood I'd take a run at is Zohra Lampert and she's not in this movie. You're safe."

"It wasn't *my* safety I was worried about. Did you find an apartment yet?"

"No. I was supposed to look at a half-dozen more of them last night, but then McCue called and I wasn't able to."

"I thought you said McCue called after midnight," she said. She was starting to wake up.

Time to flee before I was found out. "Well, I just had this feeling something was going to happen so I thought I'd better stay around. Just in case."

"I guess this means that when I get to New York, the first thing I'll have to do is to find us an apartment. If you're going to be out of town for a couple of weeks."

"That hadn't occurred to me," I said.

"I'll bet."

"Really, Chico, don't you worry about it. I'll get us an apartment."

"You'll get us some dump that no one else would live in. And what do we do in the meantime? Maybe I'll look in New Jersey," she said.

"I don't want to live in New Jersey. *They're* there, waiting for me," I said. She didn't have to ask; she knew I meant my ex-wife and the two kids, What's His Name and the girl.

"Well, we need a place to live," she said.

"We'll find a place."

"Like where? A welfare hotel?"

"We couldn't afford a welfare hotel," I said. "The city pays three thousand dollars a month for rooms in welfare hotels. We'll find someplace else."

"Two things come to mind," she said. "One. I am not staying with your mother. That woman hates me. Two. Where are you staying now?"

"With friends," I said.

"You don't have any friends."

"That explains why they're making me sleep on the front steps," I said.

There was a long pause again before she said, "This is all too complicated for me before coffee. I know you're lying but I can't figure out how or why. We'll discuss it all when we get back to New York."

"Okay," I said.

"I don't trust you when you say okay," she said.

"Go back to sleep. I'll call you when I see what's going on in beautiful upstate New York."

"Don't bring back any diseases," she said.

"No chance of that. I'm on the straight and narrow."

She snorted and I thought that I was tired of being misunderstood. Then the kid came with the rental car. Before I left, something started to nag at me, so I left Sarge a note and asked him to see what he could find out about last night's accident on Fifty-seventh Street. Then I was on my way.

Packing had been easy since I hadn't yet unpacked since getting to New York. It was the same old canvas bag that I always carry. I have more clothes than that, but they're all back in Las Vegas and Chico is probably going to throw them away because she says that I dress like a bit player on *Miami Vice*. I said, Why not the star?

and she said that I didn't dress badly enough to be the star. The star, she said, dressed like Ed Norton.

The nicest part of the drive to upstate New York was that with every boring mile I drove, I left New York City one more mile behind. Some people might think it was a pretty drive, and maybe it is, I guess, if you're into trees and pastures and farms and hillsides and lakes and stuff. I'm not. I like saloons, places that are dark, places without bugs, places without people I don't know.

Canestoga Falls was a widening in the road, with a tavern, a gas station/country store, and two other buildings that I suspected might be a firehouse and a half-room school for half-witted kids. I had to decide whether to ask for directions in the country store or in the tavern. The country store didn't stand a chance.

I ordered vodka on the rocks, but when I saw the bartender doing an engineering study to make sure the shot glass didn't contain one drop more than an ounce, I upgraded my order to a double. Somehow a double of a one-ounce shot turned out to be one and a half ounces, and I knew the Indians who had settled this area first hadn't had a chance when the bartender's ancestors arrived. They were lucky to escape with their feathers intact.

Engaging the bartender in conversation basically meant asking him questions and listening to him say yes and no. Well, not exactly yes and no. People up there kind of said "Aaaay-p" for yes and "Np" for no. After I figured that out, the conversation seemed to go easier and eventually he told me that I got to "the old Canestoga Hotel" by turning right a half-mile down the road and heading down toward lakeside. There was a sign on the roadway, he said, for "the old Canestoga Hotel," and I hadn't even had to ask him because if I had just kept driving I couldn't have missed the sign.

"Is there a *new* Canestoga Hotel?" I asked.

"Np." That meant no.

"Why do you call it 'the old Canestoga Hotel,' then?"

" 'Cause it's old. Aaaay-p. It's old."

I knew I was going to love it up there.

"You one of those movie folk?" he asked me.

"No."

"The hotel's closed, you know," he said. "Don't rent rooms no more."

"I'm not a movie folk but I've got to be there for the filming. I'm sort of involved in the production."

He thought about that for the time it took me to finish the world's skimpiest drink and said, "Production is a good thing."

He nodded his head sagely, and I said "Aaaay-p" and he said, "Aaaay-p," and since we were now such good friends, I had another drink before I left.

I spotted the hotel as I drove in the direction of the lake. With some small alterations, it might have served as home for Scarlett O'Hara. It was four stories high, white wood, and it looked like there were wings on left and right with rooms. The central section was almost all glass and I suspected that it held the lobby, dining room, staircase, and whatever. The building perched on a small knoll about two hundred feet from the lake and was surrounded on two sides and the front by high iron fences. A long driveway, bordered by high-mounted carriage lights, led to the front door.

There was a gate in the middle of the front fence. It was closed and there was a guy sitting there, sunning himself outside a little guard booth. He had a ruddy wrinkled face, thinning gray hair combed in front into an elaborate pompadour. He cocked an eye toward me as I stopped the car and rolled down the window.

"My name's Devlin Tracy," I said.

"Nice to meet you, son. My name's Clyde Snapp."

"I'm expected. Will you open the gate?"

Snapp was wearing a plaid shirt and some kind of gray work pants. Even with him sitting down, I could tell he was big. He was probably in his sixties, with big large-knuckled hands, and all in all, he looked like the kind of guy you'd pick to be with you if you had to get lost in the woods.

"You from Hollywood?" he said.

"No. Are you?"

"This place is closed. Only open for people from Hollywood."

"I'm from the insurance company. I'm supposed to be here. The producers know all about it."

"Oh, yeah. I heard you were coming," he said. He started to rearrange himself, preparatory to getting up from the wooden folding chair. "You're supposed to be the one to watch after that McCue, ain't you?"

"That's right," I said as he stood up and pushed open the heavy iron gate.

The hotel might have needed a coat of paint, but the gate needed nothing. It swung open easily, without even a squeak.

Snapp came back and stood alongside my door, hands on top of the car. "You gonna try to keep him alive, right?" I nodded and he said, "Good luck, young fella."

"That sounds ominous. Think it's going to be trouble?"

"Well," he started, and dragged it out like it was the name of a town in Wales. "That McCue fella got here this afternoon about three o'clock. Around four o'clock, I saw him crawling around on the roof."

He pointed toward the hotel, about fifty yards away. "That roof. Took a chance on breaking his neck, he did."

"What was he doing on the roof?" I asked.

"I told him to get his ass down from there. Then I asked him that. He said he always liked to see the roofs wherever he was staying. He said when they came for him, they'd likely come through the roof."

"Who the hell is 'they?' " I asked.

"That's what I wanted to know too. He said, I'd know sure enough when they came for him."

"Was he drinking?"

"Somehow I suspect so," Snapp said, nodding to agree with himself.

"Tell me, Mr. Snapp, what do you do around here?"

"Call me Clyde. I'm the caretaker. I've got to make sure that everything works for these movie folk. I'm the only one who knows how anything works."

"How long's the hotel been closed?"

"Five years. Old owner died. New owner closed it down. I been looking after things since then."

"Is there somebody inside to show me my room?"

"No," he said. "You're top floor left. I didn't know what your name was going to be, just some man from the insurance company. You're in forty-two, right next to McCue's room. I figured that might be a good thing, seeing as how you're going to keep him alive and all."

"Going to try, Mr. Snapp," I said as I put the car into gear.

"Clyde," he corrected. "Good luck, son. I wouldn't want your job."

6

"You're a bastard, Tony. You've always been a bastard."

"Yeah, but I'm a star. I'm allowed to be a bastard."

I had parked my car in front of the hotel next to a pickup truck and four other cars, one of them a white Rolls-Royce, and carried my bag into the lobby.

The voices came from a room to the right. The large sliding double doors were open and I dropped my bag and walked inside. It was a dining room with about a dozen tables that would hold four each. On one side was an eight-foot-long bar, with two stools in front of it. I figured that this was the hotel's poor excuse for a cocktail lounge.

Tony McCue was standing at the bar, facing in my direction. A tall slim woman was facing him, and even with her back to me I could see she was agitated because her shoulders were twitching up and down with nervous energy.

I realized McCue was leaner than I thought. I guess that's what cameras do to you, because every actress I ever met was fifteen pounds underweight and then when you saw her on film she wound up looking like cuddly Betty Boop.

"I should have had the part, Tony," the woman said in a voice that would frost a beer glass. "I could have done it."

"And no one would believe you in it because you're too goddamn old to play my wife."

"Old?" the woman shrieked. "I'm three years younger than you, you son of a bitch."

"That's right. And I'm in my prime and I'm a star and you're over the hill and you're Grandma Puckett. You ought to be happy, Dahlia, that you've got any part at all."

The woman snapped her head back and I saw she was draining a drink, then she slapped a martini glass down onto the bar.

"I'm going to fix you, McCue," she said, her voice softer now, but colder and somehow more threatening. "You're going to die in this film."

"I'm a star, and stars are like cats. We're allowed to die eight times before we're box-office poison." He saw me and said, "What ho. It's my keeper. Let's make him welcome."

The woman turned around, looked at me for a millisecond, and growled, "Fuck him, Tony. And you too."

She stormed past me out of the room. When she was by me, I covered my face with my arms in mock terror and McCue laughed.

He was wearing faded blue jeans and a white T-shirt that advertised "Free Mustache Rides."

He walked behind the bar and said, "Order up. I'm the bartender."

"Vodka rocks."

He put a few ice cubes in a glass for me and filled it with vodka. For himself, he crammed a glass full of cubes and then poured raw gin on top of it.

He handed me the glass, came back around, sat on the other stool, and clicked glasses. "To friendship," he said. "We're good friends, aren't we? What's your name again?"

"Call me Trace," I said. "Better friends than that woman who just left."

"That woman? You mean you didn't recognize Dahlia Codwell?"

"No. Should I?"

"Starred in a lot of movies."

"I guess I missed them," I said.

"I made twenty-seven films. You see any of them?"

"No," I said. It was true. I never went to see movies.

"I take it you're not a film fan."

"I only like Bergman and Buñuel," I said.

"They make crap," he said.

"I know. But if I get conned into going to the movies, I go to theirs and I can fall asleep and snore without bothering anybody because they're all snoring too. You have to plan ahead. Why were you climbing around on the roof today?"

McCue looked down at his drink. "This is the first time I ever had to have somebody watch over me during a film," he said. "It really hurts."

He had an interesting voice, I thought to myself. It was absolutely without accent, and when he dropped that line, "It really hurts," I thought how well he had delivered it. I also thought he was as full of shit as a Christmas goose.

"Tony, why don't we clear the air between us?"

"A wonderful idea."

"Save all the histrionics for somebody they impress, but don't try to con me," I said. "You know damned well why I'm here. Your producers have taken out a six-million-dollar policy on you 'cause they think you might drown in your shower or something. Your recent

history says that maybe they have a point. Now, you
may not want me here, and Christ knows, I don't want
to be here, but I've got the job to do. We can make it
easy on each other if we don't try to jerk each other
around. So why were you on the roof? Why do you
dive off balconies or drink booze underwater and all
that nonsense you do?"

"What if I told you that I drink because I am an artist
and I suffer for my work. That I resent being forced to
work in trivial meaningless projects like this. That in
me beats the heart of a Booth, a Kean, an Olivier, and
the pain of trivial boredom is more than I choose to live
with. What if I told you that?" His voice was eloquent
as he spoke his lines, soaring, José Ferrer doing Cyrano,
Richard Burton as Beckett. "What if I told you that?"
he repeated.

"I'd say you were trying to snow me again," I said,
"and I wish you'd stop."

"I can see you're going to be a tough case," McCue
said. "That was my best shot. It took me seven years
in London to do that."

"What do you want me to tell you? That it's wonderful acting? Okay, it's wonderful acting. But it's acting.
All I want to know is why do you act like an idiot and
are you going to act like an idiot while I'm here? Because if you are, I'm going to get a tranquilizer gun and
use it on you at night. I wasn't here two minutes and I
found out you were on the goddamn roof, playing freaking Spiderman. I don't want to have to put up with it.
And I don't want to have to put up with a lot of
playacting about it."

"All right," he said. "No more playacting. Why do
you drink?"

"I don't know why," I said.

"Right. Exactly. And I don't know why I do stupid
things. I don't want to die. I'm having too much fun.

But I think I'm deranged. I'm like a werewolf, but I don't need a full moon or any moon at all. I wander the world at night. The sun sets, I wander. I do dumb things and get myself into trouble. I don't know why, I do. Why do rock stars take drugs? Because they've done everything else, I suppose, and they're bored. All the things that keep the average man going, wanting to make a living, wanting to get laid, wanting to be able to afford a vacation in Monte Carlo, we don't have any of that incentive because we can do all those things. So what do we fill our lives with?"

"Ever try needlepoint?" I said.

"Yeah. I could do that," he said. "But what do I do next week when I'm bored with needlepoint? I'm looking for something and I don't know what it is. So I get myself in trouble. You tell me. What keeps *you* going?"

"Clean hands, a pure heart, and the knowledge that this is my work and that if I don't work, I don't eat. You asked why I drink too much, and I'll tell you. I can drink all I want because, when I do, the only person I hurt is me. But you, when you get drunk and try to kill yourself, there are a lot of other people depending on you, and one of the people you'd hurt is my client, the insurance company, and sorry, pal, you're just not allowed to do that. So no more on the roof, huh?"

He seemed to think about it as he was sipping his drink. Then he nodded and said, "Okay. If I feel the urge to climb a roof again, I'll call you first."

"Fine. I just don't want you dead on my time," I said.

"Then you'd better keep an eye on everybody else who's here too," McCue said.

"That woman's not the only one who wants to kill you?" I said.

"No. All of them do."

"Why?"

"That calls for another drink," he said. He tossed out all his ice cubes and loaded his glass up with fresh ones before splashing gin over the top of it. He refilled my glass too but let me keep the old ice cubes.

"Let's see," he said. "Dahlia's not the only one who hates me. By the way, it's not just the role she's got. She made a pass at me once and I told her I wouldn't screw her with Rent-A-Dick. Women have a way of not forgetting things like that."

"Yes," I agreed. "They take sex so seriously."

"So the screenwriter, Hard-on. He hates me."

"Hard-on?" I said.

"Arden Harden. He hates all actors because we make more money than he does. And also because we're tall. The producers hate me because I wouldn't give them a break on my fee for this film. They wanted to give me extra points out of profit, but I wouldn't do it because I told them that this film is going to be crap and there won't be any profits and that even if there were, they'd find a way to steal them. They hate me. And then we've got the director."

"Who's he?"

"Roddy Quine, this terrible old British homo who hardly knows what end of the camera to look through. He hates me ever since I told *Variety* that he was the worst director in film history."

"If he's so bad, why'd they hire him?" I asked.

"He was the best Englishman they could get for the money they were paying," he said. "Hold on, maybe there's somebody here who doesn't hate me."

"A small but significant minority," I said.

"Tami Fluff. She used to hate me because I got her axed from my last picture. But she might not hate me anymore because she's costarring in this one with me and I didn't do anything to stop it."

"Wait a minute," I said. "Tami Fluff? Tami Fluff?"

"That's her name. You never heard of her?"

"No, praise God," I said. "Where are all these people anyway? Are they all here?"

"I think so. They're in their rooms freshening up. That means they're sticking stuff in their noses probably. Hollywood has given new meaning to the phrase 'powder room.' Oh, there's somebody else here."

"Yeah?"

"My shrink," he said. "That's where I stayed last night when I left you. She's in her room working on her book. *Travels with Tony*. Don't tell her that I know about it, though. She thinks it's a secret."

He got up to make himself yet another drink, and I said, "That's pretty shabby. I didn't think that shrinks shrank and told."

"Aaaah, who cares? She figures it'll make her shrink to the stars. That's why she hangs out with me. She wants to be famous and be on the *Phil Donahue Show* so her mother in Westchester County will like her."

"You take being used pretty evenly," I said.

"I use her too," he said. "Better living through chemistry. Trace, I take pills to get up and I take pills to go to bed. I take pills to keep my heart moving. She's a doctor. She travels around with me and writes my prescriptions. It saves me from having to break into drugstores in strange towns."

He did the ritual with the ice and gin again, then sat back down and said, "You'll meet them all for dinner anyway. The old guy at the gate said seven o'clock we eat. So. Am I your first Hollywood star?"

"Yes."

"How do you like me so far?"

"I like you fine as long as you don't go climbing the roof anymore," I said. "Stick to arm-wrestling."

"That's good enough. Who knows? Maybe we'll get along."

"Maybe," I said. But I doubted it. I had the feeling that Tony McCue was going to turn out to be nothing but trouble. For one thing, he was just too open with a total stranger. It's been my experience that people who seem to be willing to tell you anything on first meeting are usually people who are trying to dictate the terms of the conversation. Sure. They'll tell you anything, just so long as it's about subjects of their choosing. Don't ask them about things they don't bring up first.

I didn't know. Maybe McCue would turn out to be the exception. I hoped so. It was going to be hard enough to nursemaid this lunatic without him playing mind games on me.

7

As often happens in the lives of troubled men with artistic souls, we stayed in the bar and never quite did get to our rooms to change for dinner.

At a few minutes to seven, Dahlia Codwell entered the room, wearing a summery white dress, walked to the bar where McCue and I were sitting, and without even acknowledging our presence, made a pitcher of martinis and carried it off to one of the dining tables.

A minute or so later, Clyde Snapp came in wheeling a serving cart. From it, he took a lot of chafing dishes filled with food and set them up on one of the long banquet tables near the bar. He left without a word to anyone.

McCue was jabbering about the impossibilities of making movies in Mexico—"their day consists of showing up late, taking a siesta, then going home early"—when I noticed him looking past me toward the door and I turned to see a tall woman with hair the color of polished pennies walking toward us, smiling.

Tami Fluff, I thought. My first taste of Hollywood. She was terrific. She wore a leg-waving bright-yellow

miniskirt and a halter top of matching material that
showed off a wonderful trim stomach and only partially
hid an equally wonderful full bustline. She had on
spiked yellow high heels, the only kind of high-heel
shoe I don't like on women, because they had straps
around the ankles and I always figure if a woman's got
good ankles, why hide them under straps? But on bal-
ance, I wouldn't fight with her over any of the ensem-
ble. The only thing wrong with it was that it seemed
designed for a precocious Lolita of a sixteen-year-old,
and this woman had to be in her late twenties. Still,
who said that actresses had to have taste?

The woman pushed by me without a glance and
tossed herself into McCue's arms. He hugged her with
his left arm and snaked his right hand down to squeeze
one of her buttocks. I figured that, in Hollywood, this
had replaced "Love you, baby" as a greeting.

Then his left hand followed suit. This, I figured,
must be a real tight Hollywood friendship if it called for
the full two-sided heinie squeeze. Then McCue disengaged and held her at arm's length with his hands on
her upper arms, just looking at her, and I knew it
wasn't too tight a relationship after all, because you
don't hold people at arm's length like that unless they're
people you want to keep at arm's length. This is a fact.

Finally McCue managed to release the woman and
said, "There's somebody I want you to meet."

She turned to me then and smiled, a lot of perfect
teeth in a perfect mouth. Every time I've met actresses
in real life, I'm always impressed by how imperfect
they are. People say that the camera is cruelly honest,
but the fact is that the makeup artist is unfailingly kind.
This woman, though, didn't need the makeup artist.
She was beautiful, all by herself, without help, and I
made a mental note to take Chico to the next Tami Fluff
movie we saw advertised.

"This is my new friend, Trace," McCue said to the woman. "Trace, this is Doctor Death."

"Pleased to meet you. Should I call you Doctor or do you prefer Death?"

"Ignore him," she said. She smiled and shook my hand, strong, dry, pleasant. "My name is Ramona. Ramona Dedley."

The shrink. This wasn't Tami Fluff at all. This was the psychiatrist who traveled with McCue.

"Is Trace your last name or first name?" she asked.

"Neither. I'm Devlin Tracy. Trace is for friends."

"Then it's Trace," she said.

"Trace is here to be my drinking buddy," McCue said as he walked around the bar and poured a glass of sherry straight up for the woman.

"For you, drinking under the buddy system is a good idea. Like scuba diving," she said.

"One should never drink alone," McCue said. "Trace is the one who got me drunk last night and made me disgusting." He then took the opportunity to make both of us fresh drinks.

Ramona and I clinked glasses and sipped.

"Doctor Death's an alchemist," McCue said.

"I thought you were a psychiatrist," I said.

McCue answered before she could. "The same thing," he said. "There's no science to what Ramona does. It's all nonsense. You ever read those stories about all the shrinks they get to come to a parole hearing to swear some guy is sane, and then they let him go and, twenty minutes later, he cannibalizes some keypunch operator eating a tuna-fish sandwich in the park? Those are shrinks. A bizarre superstition."

"Ignore him," Ramona said. "He will always be a peasant with a peasant's mind."

"Have her explain to you the lunacy at the last meeting of the headshrinks," McCue told me.

"I don't know what he's talking about," Ramona Dedley said to me.

"This is how deeply they hold their scientific principles," he said. "A couple of years ago they decided that being a homosexual wasn't really an aberration. It was just an alternate life-style, picked by choice. You know why? Because they were picketed by some gay-rights shrinks. That was then. Now their new achievement is deciding masochism doesn't really exist."

"Why's that?" I asked.

"Because the feminists forced them to. According to them, if the headshrinks say that there's a sickness called masochism, then men who beat up on women can always claim that the women wanted them to beat up on them because they were masochist sickoes. You see what I'm getting at, Trace? These people change their scientific views every time a political breeze blows, and what the hell kind of scientific views are those? Mark my words. In the twenty-first century, people are going to realize that psychiatry was no more scientific than trying to make gold out of lead. They're freaking alchemists."

I was watching Ramona while McCue was talking. She seemed to have heard it all before, because she was just listening with a bemused smile. That's one of the things people put up with who hang out with drunks; they have heard it all before because drunks always repeat themselves.

Or have I already said that?

As McCue came out from behind the bar, Ramona asked, "What actually do you do besides drinking with Tony?"

"I'm from the insurance company," I said. "We've got a policy on him and I just came up to look things over."

"Trace is going to make sure you don't kill me," McCue told her. "He's here to guarantee that you don't strap me to some couch and stuff my head with psychobabble until it bursts. 'Hollywood star Tony McCue died yesterday, his head exploded after being stuffed with bullshit by his psychiatrist, Doctor Death.' "

She snapped around. "All right, Tony. That's enough for a while. I don't like being called Doctor Death." She turned back to me. "Good luck in trying to keep him alive. I don't envy you your job." She walked away toward the entrance to the dining room.

McCue was leaning backward, his elbows reached out behind him on the bar, looking out over the dining room, which was still empty save for Dahlia Codwell, sitting at a table, sipping martinis from the pitcher she had made.

"Beautiful woman," I said about Ramona. "But you have truly pissed her off."

"Not really," he said.

"You could have fooled me," I said.

"That's because you're not an actor. You're not used to looking at how people really move," he said. "Did you see when she walked out? Straight-up walk, hip-swishing, very elegant. If she were really angry at me, she would have marched out leaning forward from the waist. No, she wasn't mad. She just had to tap a kidney and she wanted to make an interesting exit. It comes from hanging around with me too long."

"Keep it up, she may not be around too much longer," I said.

"Not before she finishes her book," McCue said. "You've got to understand, Trace. The most important thing in her life is really being a celebrity shrink. You know what kind of patients she gets now in New York? Career women who really want to be lesbians. Business executives who talk about having trouble with relationships when what they really mean is that they want to kill their wives and they won't be happy until they do.

The dullest kind of nut cases. Ramona wants to get away from all that. She's got to get to Beverly Hills, and I'm the ticket." He smiled at me and I thought I could understand the charm of a rogue like him. He had a way of smiling that made you think no one else had ever seen him smile quite so fully, quite so warmly. Maybe it was a trick actors had. I know a lot of politicians have it. Warm smile for you, only you, then clap an arm around you in a hug and, while they're hugging you, look over your shoulder to see who in the room is really important so they can dump you and get over to him.

"That's why she'll take what I dish out and still be my walking prescription pad," he said.

"Make sure she doesn't prescribe poison," I said.

"Why would she do that?"

"It'd make a great ending for the book," I said.

8

I know it's fashionable to be late for dinner, but this was getting ridiculous. It was twenty-after-seven and the Sterno was burning low under the chafing dishes and still the only one at a table was Dahlia Codwell, who was halfway through her pitcher of martinis and probably didn't care if she ever ate again.

I heard heels clicking on the floor behind me. Before I could turn around, a tiny platinum blonde ran by me.

"Tony darling," she said, and threw her arms around McCue.

"Tami, my pet," McCue said, and wrapped his arms around her. I noticed that he didn't knead her buns. Maybe they weren't real good friends, baby. Somehow I didn't think she'd mind, though, because if she had had a rhino horn attached to her pubic bone, McCue would have been impaled on it. McCue disengaged his groin and gave her the arm's-length treatment too and I had a chance to look at her.

The woman couldn't have been older than twenty-five. Her face was unlined and had never been tanned. Her complexion was cream, made up precisely to look as if she were wearing no makeup at all, but I could see a few feathers of false eyelash and some color to show off what nature had made only the hint of cheekbones. She had large eyes of a startlingly gray color that I didn't believe existed in the real world. She was wearing a silk dress—violet-colored, I guess—that fit just well enough to let you know that the body under it was perfect.

McCue winked at me.

"Oh, Tony darling, it's so good to see you again."

"It's been too long, dear," he said. "When was it? Let me think. Right. It was while you were making *Teenybop Fantasy.*"

"I didn't make *Teenybop Fantasy*," the woman said. "It was at Ma Maison. How could you forget? We danced the night away."

"Correct," McCue said. "My groin was sore for eleven days afterward. It was just before I had them turn you down for the role in *Maid of Orleans.*"

"I don't remember your turning me down," she said. Her mouth said that, I thought. Her eyes showed very clearly that she not only remembered but that she would never forget.

"Trust me," McCue said. "I did. Sort of set your career back a little too, as I remember it."

"I was just disappointed that I didn't have the chance to work with the man I regard as the greatest actor in cinema today," she said. "But the producer told me the picture was a downer and I should find a happier, more contemporary movie."

"I told him to say that," McCue said. "The real reason was that I thought—and I told him—that your being in the film would make it a laughingstock."

There was ice in her voice as she answered, "As it was, the only laughingstock about the film was the business it did. What did it gross, Tony? Exactly four-point-two million dollars, as I remember it. You made a film that should have gone directly to the *Late Late Show*, bypassing theaters entirely."

"That's true enough," McCue said agreeably. "Everybody hated it. But no one laughed. Hey, it's great to discuss old times, but we really have to look ahead to the future." He turned the young woman toward me. "There's someone here I want you to meet. This is my friend, Devlin Tracy. Friends call him Trace. Trace, this is Tami Fluff."

I wondered if I should offer my hand. Or my pubic bone. Or my throat to bite. But my decision really didn't matter because the platinum blonde just nodded at me curtly and started to turn back to McCue.

"Trace is a producer," McCue said.

As if her head were on steel springs, the woman spun back toward me and let a smile light up her face. My tonsils got warm from the wattage.

"I'm so happy to meet you, Mr. Devlin," she said.

"No, no," McCue said. "Devlin Tracy. Call him Trace. First rule of the business, Tami. Always get a producer's name right."

"Trace," she said.

"Trace is a big man in investments in New York. Handles all my big stuff. And now he's planning to make the big move into films. We were just discussing his first project now."

The woman was staring at me as if McCue weren't in the room. "How exciting," she said. "You'll love films. Somehow it seems to be the way to hold a mirror up to America, all the joy, all the sorrow. Motion pictures explain to us how we actually feel about ourselves as a nation. Don't you find that so?"

I found it hard to believe that anybody could actually speak such a line. I was going to tell her that McCue was talking bullshit, but it was tough after that speech. So I nodded.

"A mirror on America," McCue said. "Exactly so. That's what Trace is interested in, aren't you, Trace?"

"Naturally," Tami Fluff said. "He has the look of somebody serious who wants to make films that hold the mirror of truth up to America. The real America."

McCue winked at me again and said, "Tami, I'm really glad you're here to try to convince him of that because I think he's going in exactly the wrong direction. He wants to do remakes of sixties movies. A big-budget remake, for instance, of *Beach Blanket Bingo* is in development right now. Talk him out of that."

"There's nothing wrong with entertainment," Tami said seriously. "Those beach movies filled a need at the time, and perhaps America is ready for more of them." She hesitated a second. "But better-written this time, with big budgets and real talents involved."

"Forty million," McCue said. "He's got forty million for this first movie. Let me freshen that up for you, Trace," he said, and took the glass from my hands.

I wondered how I was going to extricate myself from this. Tami had moved up alongside me now and both her hands were grasping my left arm.

"How far along are you in the development process?" she asked.

"He's already got the money committed," McCue said.

"Well, if there's anything I can do . . ." Tami told me earnestly.

She looked at me as if expecting me to say something. I seemed to have paralysis of the mouth, and if she didn't stop massaging my left bicep, I was going to have trouble raising my arm in the morning.

I was saved by the sound of people coming into the dining room. There were three of them, a man leading the way. He was short but kind of bulky and wore a satin New York Mets warmup jacket. His eyes were squiny narrow, his lips a thin line, his nose short and turned up. All in all, it looked like the kind of face a man would get if he had had his head squashed, from skull to chin, in a vice. The man had tightly frizzed curled hair, which I guess is kind of fashionable in Hollywood, professional baseball, and in victims of electrocution.

Behind him walked a dark-haired woman with a frumpy-looking blouse, a dumpy-looking skirt, and a lumpy-looking body. She had a pencil behind her ears and was wearing sneakers. A taller man with thinning slicked-down hair and the kind of wattles you get from losing weight too fast in middle age brought up the rear.

The man had the face of a horse. He was wearing a flowered ascot around his neck, along with an open-throat silk striped shirt and brown tweed pants that looked as if they were cut from a fabric that had been used to wrap cotton bales.

Tami Fluff waved at the three of them, then confided to me, "That's Biff Birnbaum, the producer. Hi, Biff."

The short man in the Mets jacket scowled in our general direction.

"Oh, I guess you know him, though," she said to me.

"No."

"Okay. And the other man is Roddy Quine. He's the director, and Sheila's the girl, she's some kind of assistant producer." Tami was still squeezing my arm and the tone of her voice made it clear that this was not something she would ever do for a mere assistant producer.

Sheila went to sit at the table with Dahlia Codwell, who barely acknowledged her presence. Quine sat with Birnbaum at a table in the front of the room. Then Birnbaum got up and walked over to us at the bar.

"Come on, folks. Let's all sit down so we can get this started," he said.

He looked at me and said, "Are you the guy from the insurance company?"

Tami squeezed my arm. "This is Devlin Tracy," she said with a giggle. "He's a—"

"Yeah. I'm from the insurance company," I said.

Tami dropped my arm as if it had suddenly sprouted quills. "An insurance man?" she said, wheeling toward me.

"But a rich one, a rich one," McCue yelled. "Member of the Million Dollar Club. Want to buy a policy? He'll get you a discount."

"You prick," Tami said to me.

"I'm not an insurance salesman," I said lamely.

"What are you, then?"

"I'm an investigator," I said.

"I don't give a damn about that," she said. "You're not a movie producer."

"No," Birnbaum said. "I'm the movie producer."

"I never told you I was a movie producer," I told Tami. "He did." I pointed to McCue.

Tami glared at him. "Why are you always trying to make my life so impossible?" she demanded.

"Because you suffer exquisitely," McCue said. "Remember that scene in *T and A on Parade* when you got a run in your stocking and . . . Well, you were just wonderful. I knew then that suffering was your métier."

"If it wouldn't ruin the movie schedule, I'd ring your neck," she said, and marched away.

Birnbaum said, "If there are any necks around here to be rung, I'll ring them. Now, let's all sit down and get started. Is everybody here?" He looked around the room. "I don't see Harden."

"I refuse to eat dinner without Hard-on here," McCue said.

"Please, Tony, don't be picking on Arden this weekend. We need him."

"You need him," McCue said. He told me, "Arden Harden, the screenwriter of this moronic opus, is just possibly the most detestable person in all of Hollywood."

"The best," Birnbaum said. "Arden's the best writer in Hollywood."

"I'm beginning to believe that's like being the best epic poet in Hoboken," McCue said.

Ramona Dedley came in and sat at an empty table, so McCue and I picked up our glasses and walked in that direction.

McCue said, "I get no thanks for fixing you up with Tami?"

"That was fixing me up?"

"Certainly. If I introduced you as my bodyguard or something, she wouldn't even have talked to you, the hard little bitch. Now she's talked to you. She hates you, true, but she's talked to you and she knows who you are. So all you've got to do is find the right opportunity, abjectly apologize, and she'll come crawling into your bed like a love-struck puppy. Trust me, Trace. This is the way it works."

"I'm real glad you told me," I said. "Here I had this silly notion that she didn't like us."

"What a dumb idea," McCue said. "Everybody likes us. Especially me."

9

People shuffled around a lot. Dahlia Codwell got up and went to the bar to make herself another pitcher of martinis. It started to settle down when Roddy Quine, the director, got up and started for the food table.

"Roddy," Birnbaum snapped. The director turned around and Birnbaum patted the chair next to him. He mouthed the word "wait," and Quine went back to the table and sat down, looking like a scolded schoolboy.

"There," McCue whispered to Trace. "Now you know something about the Hollywood hierarchy. Barf Birnbaum, absolutely the worst producer in the industry, has an absolute unqualified right to boss around Quine, who also happens to be the worst director in the history of film."

"You know," I said, "you've got a lot of problems with this film. Why the hell are you doing it?"

"I couldn't resist the chance to work with so many old friends," McCue said.

Birnbaum got up and walked to the small wooden dance floor located between the bar and the tables. He looked around the room and smiled. Naturally, he had perfect teeth.

"Hi, gang," he called out. He waited as if expecting a response. Finally, there was a feeble "Hi, Biff" from a table behind me. I looked around and saw Sheila, the assistant producer, looking embarrassed.

"I'm not going to make a long speech," Birnbaum said. Codwell and McCue applauded. Roddy Quine looked startled, as if he had missed something, so he applauded too, until Birnbaum silenced him with a stare and the director went back to sulking.

"On Monday, just four days from now, Peachpit Productions is going to start filming on *Corridors of Death* right here in this hotel. Now, all us movie folk know each other and you all know me . . ."

"Barf Birnbaum," McCue whispered to me. "Dumbest producer in Hollywood."

"You said that," I said.

"It bears repeating," he said.

". . . but some of you may not know my partner— that is, personally. All of you know him by reputation. Through the years, we've had a long happy partnership. I've been handling the West Coast movie end and my partner's been handling the East Coast television part of the business. But this time, he's coming out of the closet, so to speak . . ." Birnbaum chuckled. It was the only sound in the room. ". . . and he's going to give us a hand in making our new film. Ladies and gentlemen, I'd like to present my friend and partner. You know him as Mister Talkshow, Mister Television, Mister Entertainment, but to me he's just Jack. Ladies and gentlemen, America's most beloved television personality, the Boy Next Door, Jack Scott. And his lovely wife, Pamela."

He waved a hand toward the door of the dining room as a couple walked in.

Jack Scott. I'd heard of him but I'd never heard anyone call him "Mister Television" before. He was the host of a late-night talk show and once in a while he had a television special, and it seemed his primary ability was pointing in the direction of the next act. He'd been doing the talk shows forever and every so often you'd read a story about how he always looked young and the Fountain of Youth and all that crap, but coming through the dining-room door, he looked like a tan prune with legs, wrinkled, sixty years old and showing every day of it. Chico would be impressed when I told her that; she loved gossip. The Boy Next Door? He looked like the Boy Next Door if you happened to live next door to an old folks' home.

Pamela Scott was a pretty-enough, plain woman with no makeup, no flesh tones, and hair the color of mouse fur. She was a lot younger than he was, but she didn't act younger. She walked like a woman who needed more sleep than she was getting.

Scott naturally had perfect teeth too and was showing them off. She walked behind him, looking ill-at-ease. Birnbaum was applauding their arrival.

"Let's hear it, folks, for Jack Scott and Pamela," he called out, clapping his little heart out. Behind me, there was a cascade of clapping. I didn't have to turn around this time; I knew it was Sheila proving her worth as an assistant producer.

Scott led his wife to the table; she sat down next to Quine, who seemed surprised to see her. Birnbaum sat down on the other side of her and looked toward the dance floor, where Jack Scott was rocking back and forth from foot to foot waiting for the imaginary applause in his head to die down.

"You think Barf is a dork," McCue whispered to me. "Wait until you hear this guy."

"Gee whiz, folks," Scott started out. "Whoever would

have thought, all those years ago in Albany, that here I'd be talking to such wonderful Hollywood stars as all of you"—he waved his hand around the room, taking them all in—"and a man from the insurance company. And we're getting ready to make a motion picture. Golly, I'll tell you, that's a lot of distance to come for a kid who used to sit in front of the radio and practice being a baseball announcer. 'DiMaggio swings. Click. There's a long high drive to left center field. Wertz goes back, back, back. No use. It's up and in for a home run. A four-bagger for the Yankee Clipper!' "

He paused and looked around, and Birnbaum clapped.

" 'The next batter up is Charlie Keller.' "

"Nothing succeeds like excess," McCue grunted to me.

He waited again for applause. Again Birnbaum didn't disappoint him.

Ramona leaned over to me and said, "Why is that Fluff woman glaring at you?"

I glanced over and saw the platinum blonde staring through me, like an X-ray machine.

"She just found out I'm not going to star her in my next movie," I said. "*Beach Blanket Bimbo*."

Ramona nodded and looked back at Jack Scott, who was saying what a terrific movie *Corridors of Death* was going to be.

"And sure, I want us to make money. I want us to make the greatest darned smash in the history of movies, a movie so big that we'll do a dozen sequels before we're finished. But most of all I want us to have fun. We want to have a good . . ."

He stopped in the middle of the sentence and stared over as the sliding doors to the dining room opened.

Through the doors stepped an apparition wearing a green rubber suit painted to look like the skin of a vegetable. On top of the person's head rose a stalk of rubber reeds with little balls on the end. I guess it was supposed to be an asparagus.

The creature, short and shapeless in the rubber costume, pushed the door shut behind him and stood there.

McCue jumped to his feet. "Don't worry, folks," he shouted. "Electricity will kill it."

The creature shuffled forward into the middle of the dance floor and pointed a finger at Scott, who seemed visibly to shrink.

"Good time?" the creature said. The voice was a man's voice, deep and gravelly and muffled by the rubber suit. "You say we're here to have a good time. I saw what you did to my script. You raped my script."

I touched McCue's shoulder and the actor sat down. "Arden Harden?" I asked.

"Right," McCue said. "Absolute jerk-off of the western world."

"Why is he dressed up to look like an asparagus?" I asked. I noticed that Jack Scott was sputtering and the asparagus was still shaking an accusing finger at him. I thought that it looked like the ghost of Hamlet's father. If Hamlet had been a rutabaga. Instead of a wimp.

"He's short," McCue said to me.

"That's my answer? That's why he dresses up like a finger food?"

"He likes to attract attention," McCue said. "He comes to parties dressed like the Mad Hatter, like Porky Pig, anything to make people look."

"Okay for parties," I said. "But this is like the work situation. I don't think there's much room for asparagi in the workplace. Does he show up on the sets like this?"

"He would if he thought people were ignoring him," McCue said. He called out again, "I told you, electricity will kill it." He jumped up from the table, ran across the room, and yanked an extension cord from the wall.

He came back and wrapped the end of the cord around the asparagus's right leg.

"Quick, somebody. Find a socket. Plug this in," McCue yelled, holding the end of the extension cord in his hand.

Harden swatted at it, then bent down and pulled the extension cord loose from his leg.

Jack Scott recovered, smiled, and said loudly, "As always, ladies and gentlemen, we can count on a spectacular entrance by our head writer, Arden Harden."

He tried to lead applause. The smile on Scott's face was strained and thin and he looked even older than he had entering the room. Nobody joined in the applause.

"Come on, folks. Let's hear it for Hollywood's greatest writer. Arden Harden," Scott called again. He clapped. Biff Birnbaum chipped in with some desultory clapping and Sheila started as soon as she saw Birnbaum applaud.

Scott tried to ignore the asparagus in the room.

"Okay, ladies and gentlemen, I've said what I wanted to say. I've invited us all here this weekend so we could get to know one another, to have some fun, to become one big family, before the rest of the crew arrives on Monday. Let's have fun and let's make a great movie."

Biff Birnbaum clapped wildly, jumping to his feet for a one-man standing ovation. Roddy Quine next to him looked confused.

The asparagus wheeled around, grabbed his rubberized waistband, lowered his asparagus trousers, bent over, and mooned Jack Scott.

"Mark my words," he intoned. "This movie will be a tragedy."

McCue was right; he *was* very short.

Tony McCue was still standing there, next to Harden. "You'd better believe it, folks," he called out. "That's right from the asparagus's mouth."

Harden shuffled down the length of the room, pulled

open the sliding doors, and moved through like a fast-growing ground cover. At the same moment, Clyde Snapp, the caretaker, came into the room wheeling a large silver food cart that I suspect contained desserts. If Snapp thought there was anything unusual about meeting an asparagus in his hallway, his face didn't register it.

"Dinner's buffet tonight, folks," Birnbaum said. "And let's not run out after dinner. Let's stay around and talk about our movie, *Corridors of Death*."

The asparagus stuck his head in the doorway again. "It sucks," he yelled.

10

"So you're Tracy. Good to meet you. I'm Biff Birnbaum."

"I know. We met at the bar before."

Birnbaum gave me a toothy grin. I wanted to ask him about his tightly curled hair. Did he have to put rollers in it at night when he went to bed? I wonder about things like that.

He said, "Sorry. You know how it is. You meet so many people in so short a time."

I looked around the room at the seven or so people there, all of whom Birnbaum had met before, and I wondered who he might have confused me with.

"Sure. I know how it is," I said. "I have trouble remembering people's names too, Riff."

"Biff. It's Biff. Biff." He was short but seemed to have large shoulders somewhere under the New York Mets jacket. He had taken the only free seat at our table, so Sheila, who had followed him over, had to bring a chair from another table so that she could sit with us.

She had stringy hair, dark and dirty-looking, and wore no makeup. I don't know if it would have done much good. Her features were ordinary, and the best she could hope for would be for someone to say she was nice-looking. Still, I suspected that in New York she would have tried. She would have worn makeup and done her best. But in Hollywood, she was surrounded by beauties, so I guess she had just surrendered.

"I'm Sheila Hallowitz," she told me. She shook my hand firmly. "I'm the assistant producer."

Birnbaum had turned his back on me already and was talking to Tony McCue. "So, Tony, are you ready to make the best picture of your life?"

"Don't tell me we're going to scrap this one and do a remake of *Quo Vadis?*"

"Very funny," Birnbaum said, but he was not amused. "I'm afraid we're paying too much to change directions now. I just wanted to ask you to take it a little easy on Arden. He's excitable. You know how screenwriters get."

McCue shook his head. "You're sure not paying me enough to make me be nice to Hard-on. The man's an imbecile. He needs help. Talk to Ramona. He needs a shrink. Or a gardener. That's it, Barf. I've got it. Get him to wear his asparagus costume out into the yard and I'll hire somebody to run over him with a lawn mower."

Birnbaum sighed. "We need him, Tony. There's a lot of work to do on the script still. If you remember, you're the one who said that."

"Yes. And I'm also the one who told you you ought to get a real writer in, not this lunatic." McCue poured Birnbaum a glass of straight gin from the bottle he had brought over from the bar. "Have a drink. It'll cheer you up," he said.

"Never drink," Birnbaum said. He pushed the glass past him. "Here, Sheila, you drink it." He never bothered to look at her.

Dutifully she picked it up and sipped at the straight warm liquor. She made a face and tried not to choke.

Birnbaum tried a different approach. "I think we're going to have a good time here," he told McCue. "Even the dinner wasn't bad."

"I think we're going to have a perfectly shitful time here," McCue said.

Birnbaum took a deep breath and turned to me as if trying to find someone friendly to talk to.

I said, "Any special reason why you wear the Mets jacket?"

"Just a habit," he said. "I don't ever want to forget that I'm from New York."

I thought about New York for a moment and said, "Why not?"

"Street kids. We learn survival in New York. That's the most important skill you need in Hollywood."

"Oh, horseshit," McCue said. He was good and drunk now and smiling and really getting into it. "You grew up in freaking White Plains. The only time you saw a New York street was when your high-school class passed through on the way to visit the Planetarium."

Birnbaum said, "My heart's on the New York streets."

"Your ass may be too if this movie isn't any better than your last ones. How many flops in a row is it now?"

Sheila Hallowitz gently returned a sip of gin to the glass, wiped her mouth, and said, "Biff's last picture earned out. It's turning a tidy profit, from our reports."

"It might make four dollars," McCue said, "and that's only if the gross in Hong Kong is good."

"We're a smash in Europe," she mumbled, looking down at the table.

"Trace, for your edification, that means that people haven't yet started throwing up in the theaters," McCue explained to me. "That's what these people call a smash.

They spent twenty million to make a film and it grossed five million in the States. All because they forgot to get a script that made any sense. And now they're doing the same thing here. They hired this exhibitionist asparagus. He's written a script that's incomprehensible and they didn't know it until I told them."

"Artists," Birnbaum said to me. "They're all like this." He rose from the table, and as if they were connected at the hip, Sheila Hallowitz rose too.

"Well, Tony," Birnbaum said, "we'll be talking about this a lot more this weekend, I'm sure. Tomorrow you and I will walk out around the property and sight up some good shooting locations. Excuse me, I have to find the men's room."

With Sheila in tow, he left before McCue could respond. He looked unhappy and Sheila looked miserable. She seemed to be the kind of woman born to walk three paces behind and one to the left.

"Is everything that bad?" I asked McCue.

He poured himself another drink. "Worse," he said. "That cretin is what's wrong with Hollywood today."

"This is Jack Scott's first film?" I asked, and McCue nodded.

"So far as I know."

"Maybe he came to help out. So that Birnbaum didn't screw things up again," I suggested.

McCue croaked out a dry chuckle. "Well, that's really the stupid leading the stupid," he said. "Scott's no prize either. His talk show is flopping and his last three television specials vanished without ever being seen. All he can do here is make things worse. If that's possible."

There was something still gnawing at me. I again asked McCue, "Why are you making this film if you hate it so much?"

"I'm on a loan-out. I owed a studio a picture, so the studio lent me to Scott to make this turkey."

"Don't you big stars have script approval or whatever they call it?"

"I gave it up this time so the studio wouldn't sue me over some problems with the last film. No use, Trace. I'm stuck with this detritus." McCue stood up and said, "I've got to go to the little boy's room." He shuffled away from the table, halted five steps away, turned around, and came back for his glass. "In case I get delayed," he said with a smile, then stumbled away again.

"Do you realize that we're the only two sane people in this whole place?" Ramona Dedley said to me. Her eyes looked a little tired. She had started off by refusing drinks, but McCue had worn her down and she had been putting her own hurting on the gin bottle.

"And I'm not too sure of me," I said.

"You'll keep a close eye on Tony, won't you?" she said.

"It's what I'm paid to do. Why?"

"I've just got bad vibes about this film," she said.

"Bad vibes? Is that a professional judgment?"

"No. Just a hunch," she said. "I have to go up to my room to freshen up a while. Tell Tony where I am, will you?"

"Sure," I said. I offered her a hand, but she waved it away and got heavily to her feet by herself. She started toward the door in that lurching walk that tipsy people have, especially if they're inexperienced, with the body tilting forward from the waist. It's like running downhill, but the problem is you can neither stop nor change directions. I've discovered over the years that this is the cause of most traffic collisions with other pedestrians. When I do drunk-walking, I always lean backward. I can't see my feet in case I trip over something, but I can stop fast.

Even lurching, Ramona Dedley looked sexy. She bar-

reled through the open doors of the dining room, almost
knocking down a small young man wearing a heavy
college-style white sweater with big block letters on the
front: F U.

He looked around the dining room and I looked at
him. He was hardly five feet tall and wore horn-rimmed
glasses that made him look like a praying mantis. His
features were pleasant enough, but there was a petulant
downturn to his mouth that was close to a scowl.

He walked over and sat down at my table, facing me.

"I guess I can talk to you," he said. "You only look
half-stupid."

"Appearances can be deceiving," I said.

"Who are you?" he said.

"Devlin Tracy. I'm with the insurance company. Who
are you?"

"I'm Arden Harden. I'm the screenwriter."

"I didn't recognize you without hollandaise sauce," I
said.

"I've been outside a long time. I saw you talking to
Barf Birnbaum. Did he say anything about my script?"

"He loved it," I said. "He said it was the greatest
scenario since *Gone With the Wind*. Or since *Chitty
Chitty Bang Bang*. I don't remember, but he loved it."

"Then why's he keep changing it?" Harden said.

"I didn't ask him."

"He's changing everything. You know why they
bought my script in the first place?"

"Because you're such a pleasant guy everybody wanted
to do you a favor?" I suggested.

"No. They bought it because they wanted the title.
Then you know what they did first thing? They changed
the title. I wrote *Death Stalks the Corridors*. It was a deep
psychological study of a twisted mind. Now, they're
going to call it *Corridors of Death* and make it into a
goddamn mystery. Why?"

"It's a mystery to me," I said.

"That's right. Me too. But Barf and that serving girl of his, Sheila Half-wits, and that horse-faced excuse for a director are jerking around, changing my words. It's the old Hollywood syndrome. Everybody wants to pee in the soup. Did you know that?"

"Remind me not to order the soup," I said.

"It's an old Hollywood joke. They hire the best chef in the world to make the greatest soup. Somebody says at lunch that it's wonderful and the producer and director both agree, but before they eat it, they both stand up and pee in it because they want to give it their own personal touch. They're peeing on my script. Who are you anyway?"

"Devlin Tracy. I thought we had already agreed on that."

"You sell insurance or something?"

"No. I'm here to nursemaid Tony McCue for a while. Keep him alive."

"They think somebody's going to murder him?"

"It's more like maybe he'll drink himself to death," I said. "Or fall out a window or something."

"Bet on murder," Harden said. "I'd like to kill him. What'd he say about my script?"

"He thinks it's shit."

"That's because he's not wearing leotards and a sword. That asshole wants to keep remaking *Robin Hood*."

"Who'd want to kill him?" I asked.

"Everybody," he said.

"You?"

"Naturally. He changes one of my lines, I'll cut his goddamn throat with a butter knife. Slow and painful."

"Would you like a drink?" I asked.

"I don't drink," he said.

"Dinner's already been taken away. Did you eat?"

"Not any crap they serve here. I travel with my own

food. Grains and things. I don't like hotel shit. Why are you being nice to me?"

"I thought it was my Christian duty."

"What's a Christian doing on a movie shoot? Are you a Christian?"

"On Saturdays I'm a Christian. On Sundays, I'm a Jew," I said. "That way I can avoid church all week."

"Good thinking," Harden said.

"Who else would want to kill McCue?" I asked.

"I told you. Everybody."

"Even Birnbaum?"

"Especially Barf. You know what his real name is? It's Irving. That tells you something about his taste. If he wanted to change his name, he could have called himself Irv. Irv Burns or something. That would be a good name. Biff Birnbaum is a joke."

"But he wouldn't kill."

"Of course he would. McCue held him up for two million dollars for this picture and its going to be a dud and Barf hates anybody who holds him up for money."

"Why's it going to be a dud if you wrote it and it's so great?" I asked.

"First of all, they're changing it. But even if they didn't, it'd stink because Barf can't make movies. He turned down a project of mine two years ago because 'Nobody does martial-arts movies' and then *Karate Kid* came out and grossed over a hundred million dollars. I want water. Why don't you have water at this table?"

"There wasn't much call for it with McCue and me here," I said.

"You're another boozer?"

I shrugged. He looked at me in disgust and reached over to an adjoining table for a pitcher of water and a glass. He had the smallest hands I'd ever seen on a man.

"You were talking about Birnbaum," I said.

"Yes. He can't make movies even a little bit. He's too

cowardly to make like a *Rambo* and too stupid to make *Dumbo*, so he's going to take my beautiful script and turn it into *Limbo*. I can see it coming."

"Maybe that's why Scott showed up for this film," I said.

Harden waved a hand in dismissal. "Another bean-bag. Do you know that dimbulb started a clothing company so people could dress like him, with those sappy tweed jackets and shit? Now you know why I dress like an asparagus. Anything's better than dressing like him. Anyway, that company went broke and then he wrote his life story, a pail of illiterate gruel, and it sold about four copies, and his talk show on television stinks and the guy's a fucking loser."

"Birnbaum called him a triple-threat man before," I said mildly.

"Yeah. He lies, he cheats, and he steals."

"Does he hate McCue too?" I asked.

"He ought to."

"Why?"

"Because everyone ought to," he said.

"Tami Fluff seemed to like McCue enough," I said.

Harden's eyes squinted and he looked real angry. "You know why they call them starlets?" he asked me.

"No. Why?"

"Because piglets was already taken. Of course she acts like she likes McCue. She wants to stay on the picture."

"She's starring in it, isn't she? Could McCue get her fired?"

"Of course he could. And that's another thing about Birnbaum. He has no sense about who's right for a part. The part I wrote calls for the female lead to speak lines like a real human being. He had no right to sign up that twat for the part."

"You ought to think about giving up Hollywood," I said. "You don't sound happy."

"Where else can I make a quarter of a million dollars for two weeks' work?" he asked. "Barf really said he liked my script?"

"That's what he said," I answered.

"I'm going over and tell him he's a liar." He stood up and said to me, "It's going to be a miracle if we get through this weekend without a murder."

"Pray for miracles," I said.

He walked over to the table where Birnbaum and Sheila were talking to Dahlia Codwell. The actress had slowed down and was still working on her second pitcher of martinis. She didn't look too bad. There are some people who drink like that. One half-drink and they get to a certain level of tipsy and then they stay there, no matter how much more they drink, until they pass out. Hollywood did create some ferocious drinkers, I thought. Codwell and McCue were both world-class.

Harden sat down and I turned away to see Jack Scott motioning me politely over to the empty chair at their table. I grabbed my drink and walked over and Scott got up and shook my hand.

"I'm Jack Scott."

"Devlin Tracy."

"And this is my wife, Pamela. And this is Roddy Quine, who's going to direct *Corridors of Death*."

Pamela Scott looked at me shyly, then looked away. She had the unhappy kind of look on her face that God gives to certain people who were created only to suffer. Quine nodded but did not offer a handshake.

"I just wanted to tell you that I'm glad your company was able to send you up here," Scott told me.

"Protecting the investment," I said.

"Exactly. And he needs some protecting, that's obvious."

"How's that?" I asked.

"You've watched Tony tonight. His drinking is getting worse and worse."

"He seems to handle it," I said.

Scott shook his head. "When he used to drink normally, he did crazy dangerous things. Now he's drinking worse and I'm afraid of what he might do to himself." He gave me a smile. Up close, he was as wrinkled as the hands of a bathed baby. "Well, fella, I'm just as glad you're here to keep an eye on him. He's not really well, you know. Last night we had dinner with him in New York and he got real drunk. Then he wouldn't go home. Biff and I were real worried about him. Keep an eye on him. Please."

"I'll try my best."

"Is this your regular work? Are you a policeman?" Scott asked.

"I work for a private-detective agency," I said. "We do a lot of work for the insurance company."

"No special background in things like this?" he said.

I shrugged. "I know something about drinking."

"Well, try to keep an eye on him. It's no secret that without Tony we don't have a picture."

"I didn't think anybody in Hollywood was indispensable," I said.

"Some actors get hot, and Tony's one of them. Mystery movies generally don't make it with the public, so we're hoping Tony's appeal can get this one over the top. Gee, I hope so. We're going to have a wonderful movie." He smiled at me again. It was the kind of smile that came from a guy who had trained himself to smile at the end of every six sentences.

It occurred to me that I had not yet seen Roddy Quine, the director, say one word to anyone the entire evening.

So I asked him, "How do you like the script, Mr. Quine?"

He took a deep breath before answering. Maybe no one had ever spoken to him before. He opened his mouth and showed me teeth that would have made Secretariat proud.

"The magic of movies," he said.

He looked pleased with himself, as if that were an answer to my question.

Scott looked anxiously around the room. "Where is Tony, by the way?"

"He was going to the men's room," I said.

"That was a long time ago," Scott said.

"Maybe he fell in," Quine said, and started guffawing, showing all his teeth, looking, sounding, and acting like the imbecile end product of too much British inbreeding. "Hee, hee, hee." He actually giggled.

I saw Tami Fluff step into the doorway of the dining room. She looked around, right past me, but when her eyes reached the table next to mine, she seemed to change her mind and walked away from the open doors.

A moment later, Dahlia Codwell walked out of the room.

I stood up. "I'm going to see where Tony is," I said.

"Attaboy," Scott said. "Always on the job. Keep our movie alive, Mr. Tracy."

11

McCue was not in the men's room. I looked inside the two unlocked stalls to make sure he had not fallen asleep inside them.

As I came out of the men's room, which was down a little hallway across from the main dining room, I saw Dahlia Codwell leave the ladies' room farther down the hall and turn the corner toward the dining room.

Before I reached the other corridor, I heard a voice and stopped to listen.

"Hello. May I call you mother?"

"You may call me Miss Codwell, you tart."

"What's the matter?" the first voice answered. It was soft and buttery and belonged to Tami Fluff.

"The matter, you little tramp, is that while I may be working in the same film you are infesting, I have no inclination to be your friend or confidante. I saw you making up to that drunken bastard McCue earlier tonight. Tell me you weren't trying to fatten your role at the expense of mine."

"I wasn't," Tami answered.

"I doubt that."

"It's true. I was telling Tony how happy I was to be working on a film with two people, like you two, whom I respect and admire so much."

"Save the valedictories for your death scene," Dahlia snapped back. "You still die in this movie, don't you? Or have you slept your way into immortality?"

"I don't know what I've done, Miss Codwell, to offend you, but whatever—"

"You offend me by being alive. Your vacant face offends me. Your ridiculous name offends me. Your nonexistent nose offends me. Everything about you offends me. All I want from you is that you remember that you are a piece of meat who has somehow fucked her way into my motion picture. But meat is plentiful, and in the next film be sure that you will be replaced by another side of beef."

"It's very sad, Miss Codwell," Tami said evenly. I could smell the perfume the women wore. It was a ripe, overpowering smell. Tami said, "All I had hoped for on this film was that I could learn something about my craft from working with such skilled professionals as you two. I will learn, Miss Codwell, whether you want me to or not. As for my being a piece of meat, I'm sorry you feel that way, but it isn't true. I was chosen for this part because I can act. And because I'm young enough to play it."

"Why, you bitch! Are you implying that I'm too old to have played your part?"

"The decision wasn't mine, Miss Codwell," Tami said. "You could convince me, I'm sure. You should have convinced the people who make those decisions."

"It's not possible when you've got yourself opened like the hold of a ship to anyone who comes along."

"Good evening, Miss Codwell," Tami said.

I plopped down into a chair as Tami turned the corner into the hallway leading to the rest rooms. There was a triumphant smile on her face, a happy gleam in her eyes. Then she saw me and her face soured.

"It's not my day," she said. "First you, then her. Do you always hang around eavesdropping?"

"I wasn't eavesdropping. I just didn't want to barge in. And for what it's worth, I think she was cheap-shotting you," I said.

"Thank you for that anyway, Tracy." She started to brush by me toward the ladies' room, then stopped and smiled again. It was a wonderful smile. "I really singed her ass, didn't I?" she said.

"Third-degree burns over ninety percent of her body," I said.

"Good. I wasn't lying anyway. I'll put up with her crap. And I'm going to watch her and pick her brains and learn everything I can about this business. Do you have a cigarette?"

"Sure," I said, and realized that nobody but McCue and I had been smoking in the dining room. Ahhh, sweet Hollywood.

"Is she that good an actress?" I asked.

"Good?" Tami said, inhaling deep on the cigarette. "She stinks. She couldn't act her way into a high-school Thanksgiving show. The only thing she ever did was get a star to fall in love with her and marry him and wait for him to die. She never could act. She just looked like she could. The only acting she ever did was pretending she liked giving blowjobs, from what I've heard. And she accuses *me* of sleeping my way onto this picture."

"If she's so lousy, what do you want to learn from her?" I asked.

"How to steal the camera. You watch her, any scene she's in, and it looks like she's the only person in it. That's a trick, and I'm going to figure out how she does it, the old bitch."

"Good for you, Tami," I said.

"I'm going to be around this business for a long time," she said.

"I have a hunch you're right."

"If you ever do get rich and produce a movie, look me up. I might be interested."

"I don't know if I could afford you," I said.

"You never know," she said. "Try me." She stubbed out the cigarette and wiggled into the ladies' room.

12

I grabbed my canvas bag from the corner near the front door and decided to go upstairs to find my room. Clyde Snapp had told me that I was next door to Tony McCue. Maybe he was up there.

At the bottom of the steps, a room chart was posted on the wall. I saw that the Scotts, Roddy Quine, and Dahlia Codwell had the first floor of rooms. On the second were Birnbaum and Sheila in a suite, Ramona, and Tami Fluff. I was on the top floor with McCue and Arden Harden, the screenwriter.

As I walked up the steps, I realized I wasn't really much of a detective. I had been at the hotel for four hours or so and I hadn't seen anything except the dining room and the men's room in the hall. There could have been a battalion of Libyan murderers hanging around upstairs and I never would have known. Well, what the hell, I thought. I didn't ever want to be a detective and I wasn't going to be one and I was only going through the motions just to keep Chico quiet until I found something I was better at, if such a thing existed.

There was no elevator and a sweeping staircase, fifteen feet wide, led from the lobby up to the first floor of rooms. There were only a couple of dozen rooms in the hotel.

One flight up, the staircase opened to two hallways. On the left side of the stairs there were four rooms. There were probably an equal number on the right side, over the dining room, but I couldn't tell because the hallway had been sealed off with a temporary plasterboard wall that was posted with a sign that read, DO NOT ENTER. AREA UNDER CONSTRUCTION.

It was the same on the next floor of rooms. I heard a loud thump down the hallway to the left and then I heard a grunt. I was curious, so I put down my bag and walked down the hallway. The last door on the left was open and I looked inside to see Biff Birnbaum, stripped to a pair of gym shorts, wrestling with a heavy barbell. He yanked it up over his head, locked his arms, then saw me and dropped the weights down onto a pair of couch pillows.

He grinned his perfect grin. "I try to lift every night," he said. "It's good for working off the tension."

"Tension? Here? I hadn't noticed any," I said, but Birnbaum seemed disinclined to talk, so I left him lugging the weights.

On the next floor up, the top floor, McCue had the two-room suite directly above Birnbaum's. Mine was a single room next to his. Number 42. I put down my bag and walked over to the entrance to McCue's suite and listened. The heavy sound of snoring vibrated the wood of the door. Either Tony McCue was sleeping it off or he had bought a chain saw and was practicing on the legs of the bed.

I closed my door and noticed that there was no keyhole for a lock. The doors locked from the inside with dead bolts. When you were in, you could keep the world out. But when you went out, anybody could go traipsing about your room. It'd never work in Manhattan, I thought, but what the hell. Maybe the people were different up here in the fresh air.

I dumped all my stuff into one of the drawers and stuck the canvas bag in a closet. I knew I had a bottle of vodka, so I started rooting around in my clothes, looking for it. I found the pint bottle and a couple of packs of cigarettes and I reminded myself to buy more tomorrow because I didn't think there was going to be a cigarette machine in this hotel.

There was no refrigerator or ice tray or anything like that in the bathroom, so I poured the vodka, warm and neat, and lay on the bed smoking.

Then I noticed a little door in the wall, over the dresser. I got up and tried to open it, but it was screwed shut and there was paint over the screw head. I guessed it was an old-fashioned dumbwaiter that used to connect from the basement to the guest rooms. It was the old way of getting hot water from the basement up to the rooms before hot-water systems were installed. It was probably used too for packing garbage down to the basement and maybe even for hoisting food up to the rooms. And it was also probably a great way for mice to get all over the building without having to climb the stairs.

I lay back down, smoked awhile, and then lifted the bedside telephone. I was surprised to get an immediate dial tone and then I remembered it wasn't likely that this place would have a switchboard operator. Probably direct lines had been pumped into the rooms while the movie shooting was going on.

As I dialed, I could hear McCue snoring next door. Some people were annoyed by snorers and couldn't sleep when they heard the noise. I'm not one of them. My father brought me up believing that the best defense is a good offense, and I may just be the most offensive snorer in the world, especially when I'm drinking. Wait until I went to sleep. I'd knock McCue right out of bed.

Chico answered on the first ring.

"Hi. Devlin Tracy, boy bodyguard here."

"Good," she said. "I was just in the kitchen fixing dinner. Why are you calling so early? What is it, about ten o'clock there?"

"About that," I said. "The subject has gone to sleep. If you listen carefully, you can hear him snoring next door. So I've decided to turn in too. It's part of the new me."

"The old you was good enough, you know," she said. "So come on, fill me in on all the Hollywood gossip. Who else is there? Did anyone have their clothes ripped off yet and get thrown in the pool? Come on, dammit, talk."

"There's no pool. It's freezing here and even a starlet would think twice about jumping into the lake here. It's got ice on it, I think."

"So you promised me the dirt on McCue. Let's have it. What's he really like?"

"He's a man like all of us. He just wants to be loved and understood."

"And because he isn't, he drinks, right?"

"How'd you know that?" I asked.

"I hear it a lot," Chico said. "You don't have any dirt for me?"

"Okay," I said. "McCue's a wild man. He drinks worse than I do. He's a pill-popper too. He travels with his own shrink, who's the best-looking woman here, even if she does dress like a Forty-second Street hooker."

"Stay away from her," Chico said. "Shrinks screw like minks."

"Mink," I said. "Mink is plural."

"Mink doesn't rhyme, though. This isn't much of a report. Who else is there?"

"Well, there's Jack Scott, America's favorite sixty-year-old Boy Next Door, and his wife. He looks like a prune and she looks like she could use prunes. Are you taking notes?" I asked.

"I don't have to. I remember everything. What else?"

"We've got Dahlia Codwell. She hates McCue because he calls her Granny Puckett. She wanted to play his wife in this picture but he said she was too old, and now she's playing the wife's mother. She's pissed. She thinks the actress who got the job is a tart."

"Is she?"

"I don't know. She's pretty smart. She called me a prick already."

"Very fast learner. Who is she?"

"Tami Fluff. I don't know who she is," I said. "I never go to movies."

"I know. I always have to go alone. Tami Fluff. She's the new hot thing. Stay away from her. What's she like?"

"At first, you think she's got all the brains of a cotton ball, but I think there's something going on between the ears."

"Why'd she call you a prick?"

"Because McCue told her I was a producer and she came on to me and then she found out I wasn't."

"Lying will always get you into trouble," Chico said.

"It gets you into panties too, sometimes," I said. "Anyway, she and Codwell hate each other, I guess. And Tami—"

"Tami now, is it?"

"Miss Fluff. Miss Fluff hates . . . I can't call anybody Miss Fluff."

"Tami. Get on with it," Chico said.

"Tami is pissed at McCue because he got her turned down for a role in a picture he did, something about Joan of Arc."

"Right. He was nominated for an Academy Award for that. So was his costar, I think."

"Well, Tami's unhappy with that. I think. Let's see. Who else is mad at my client?"

"I don't know. Who?"

"Biff Birnbaum, the producer."

"You're kidding," Chico said.

"No, I'm not. Biff Birnbaum is the producer of this thing. They call it *Corridors of Death*, by the way. He's mad at McCue because Tony held him up for too much money and Tony hates the script and says the picture's going to be crap. Oh, yeah. The screenwriter hates McCue too. His name's Arden Harden. McCue calls him Hard-on."

"I've read a couple of his books. A modest talent at best," Chico said.

"He's ticked at everybody because they're making his screenplay into a mystery. Oh, and there's this woman named Hallowitz. Harden calls her Half-wits. I don't think she likes McCue 'cause he's always picking on Birnbaum."

"Who is she, though?" Chico asked.

"The assistant producer."

"Skip her. Gossip about assistant producers isn't worth anything."

"There's the director. Roddy Quine. You ever hear of him?"

"Yeah. He made a couple of spy movies, I think."

"A horse's ass to go with his horse's face. McCue says he's the worst director in the world."

"Why is McCue making this movie if everything's so bad?" Chico asked, and I thought again how quick she was, most of the time, to cut through the nonsense and get to the heart of a matter.

"He's stuck with it on some kind of contract thing. I

don't understand it. He said when it's done, he may take an ad in *Variety* and tell people to stay away."

"That should endear him to everyone," Chico said.

"Doctor Death doesn't know why he does things either," I said.

"Who's Doctor Death?"

"Ramona," I said.

"Who the hell's Ramona?"

"The shrink. Her name's Dedley or something, and McCue calls her Doctor Death. He travels with her so she can prescribe drugs from him in strange places. This place qualifies."

I told her about the hotel and the bar in town. She told me that she had found the deed to the condominium taped to the bottom of a dresser drawer.

"Why'd you put it there?" I said.

"I didn't put it there, you imbecile. You did. For safekeeping, I suppose."

"It worked. It kept it safe till now," I said. I didn't remember ever putting anything on the bottom of a drawer. "Anybody interested in subletting?"

"A lot of people," she said. "I think half the Hoboken Fire Department has been up here already to look at the place. You'd be amazed at how many people come to Las Vegas and really think they'll be able to make a living gambling."

"I wonder if we should warn the casinos," I said.

"I think they'll survive without our help."

"How long?" I asked.

"How long what?"

"So long, Oolong, how long you gonna be gone?"

"No change. Ten days maybe. Why?" she said.

"Because I'm only going to stay here until you come to New York and then I'm bailing out. This is a waste of time."

"Why? You said everybody wants to kill McCue. Maybe somebody will."

"Go ahead," I snarled. "Try it. Make my day."

"That's the lousiest Clint Eastwood I ever heard."

"That's because it was John Wayne. Hurry up, will you?" I said. "You get to New York and we can look for an apartment."

"I knew it was going to fall to me eventually to do that," she said. "You'd better be thinking of where we're staying until we find an apartment. Your mother's place is out, O-U-T, out. The last time we were there she accused me of breaking a plastic spoon with Virginia Beach printed on it. Listen, are you getting all these conversations on tape? I'd love to hear them."

"No. I left my tape recorder home. It's the new me."

"You're a pain in the butt. Call me tomorrow," she said.

I hung up and lit another cigarette and smoked awhile before I realized something was wrong. What was it?

And then it hit me. I couldn't hear Tony McCue snoring anymore.

13

I waited for a moment outside the door of McCue's suite. I heard nothing from inside and then I tried the door. If it was locked, that meant McCue was inside because there was no way to lock the door from the outside. But the door opened easily.

I found the light switch and flipped it on. I was inside a small living room, with a dining table, a small refrigerator, a couch, but like my room, no television set. There was a large old Gestapo-style radio in a corner and there were paintings on the walls, not the usual Holiday Inn prints but large oils of pastoral scenes, stuff Chico told me once was from the Hudson Valley School of Painting. That meant less than nothing to me. I just envied McCue his refrigerator.

There was a locked dumbwaiter door in his wall too.

I walked into the bedroom, but the bed was empty and still made. I guess McCue must have dozed off on the couch in the other room for me to have heard his snoring so clearly. Hidden in this bedroom behind that heavy door, even he could snore without being heard.

I looked inside the bathroom just to make sure that

the dippo wasn't scuba diving in his bathtub, but it was empty. He was a more organized sort of traveler than I was because his shaving gear was neatly arranged on the shelf next to the sink. A half-dozen vials of drugs with prescription labels on them were neatly arranged behind the faucets. I glanced at them, but they all were capsules with little grains in them and they all looked like Contac to me. The physician's name on each of the vials was Dr. R. Dedley.

But where the hell was McCue?

That was one big question. The other one was, Why did he rate a two-room suite with a refrigerator when I, the representative of the great insurance industry of the United States, had only a single room and not an ice cube in sight?

I tossed on a jacket and went downstairs. The dining room was dark and empty. There was a small night-light on over the bar, and on one of the tables were urns of coffee and hot water and cups and tea bags and sugar and cream and a pile of individually wrapped Danish pastries.

People must go to bed early around here, I thought as I looked at my watch—the old-fashioned kind with hands dipped in luminous paint that causes radiation poisoning of the wrist—because it was only eleven o'clock.

I thought about having a piece of Danish, changed my mind, and was halfway out the door when a voice called to me out of the darkness.

"Tracy."

It was a woman's voice, and I walked into the darkness of the dining room and found Dahlia Codwell at a table, still drinking martinis from a pitcher. The pitcher was full and cold with sweat.

"I thought it was you," she said in her husky whiskey voice. "Birnbaum says you're with the insurance company."

"Right. Trying to keep McCue alive."

"God, and I always thought there were some things people wouldn't do, even for money," she said. Without asking, she poured a drink from her pitcher into a glass and pushed it to me. "Have a drink. It's fresh, I just made it."

"Have you seen McCue?"

"He'll be right back," she told me. "Sit down."

I sat and sipped the drink.

"So what do you think of our cozy little Hollywood family?" she asked me.

"I don't know. I wasn't ready for people dressing up like asparaguses," I said.

"Arden is harmless. He just likes attention and he likes to play Cassandra. It's the refuge of the witless."

"Why witless?" I asked.

"Did you know, Mr. Tracy, that ninety percent of all movies take a bath?"

"No, I didn't know that."

"It's true. So if you predict that any movie is going to be a flop, you've got a ninety-percent chance of being right. It doesn't require any thought or brains. That's what Arden does, and nine out of ten times he's right and then people say how smart he was to predict it."

"Are you trying to tell me that this movie isn't as bad as everyone says it's going to be?" I asked.

"Nine chances out of ten it'll flop," she said.

"If everybody knows that about movies, why bother making them?"

"Because it's a paycheck for everybody: actors, directors, crew, trollops who think they're actresses. And even on a flop, the producers steal a lot of money, so they wind up all right. And if it's that one out of ten that makes it, then everybody can get very rich. Everybody keeps coming back for the dream. That's the way it is."

She refilled her glass and I said, "I'm very impressed, Miss Codwell."

"By what?"

"By how much you can drink without collapsing."

"It's like getting to Carnegie Hall. It takes practice, practice, practice."

"You said McCue said he'd be right back. Did he go to the men's room?"

"I don't know. I didn't see him," she said.

"Excuse me?" I said.

"I lied. I saw him going outside before and I heard his car start up. I wanted to give him a head start just in case he was on his way to get killed."

"Thanks a lot, lady."

"You might be upset, but the world will be better off," she said.

I went out on the front steps. Sure enough, the white Rolls-Royce was gone. The son of a bitch had sneaked out.

It was only the end of September, but it felt like the new Ice Age had already started. It was freezing. Unfortunately, planning ahead wasn't one of my strong suits, and there was no coat in my room. I was just going to have to be cold.

There was a guard at the gate and I rolled down the window and said, "Did McCue say where he was going?"

The guard was young and potbellied, with a mustache that hung down too far at the corners for my taste. Generally I find that people with Fu Manchu mustaches are people of low moral caliber.

He came over and looked inside the car, past me. "Which one are you?" he asked.

"What do you mean?"

"I don't recognize your face." He craned his neck trying to look on the floor of the back seat.

"I'm not an actor. I'm McCue's goddamn nursemaid,"

I said. "Now, if you're finished inspecting the upholstery, where the hell did he go?"

"Sorrrrry," the young man said, and I decided to get out of the car and hit him. Then I decided not to, just in case he was tough. He said, "McCue asked me where the nearest cocktail lounge was."

"What'd you tell him?"

"I told him New York City. He wasn't going to find no cocktail lounge up here. He said something like, Young man, a watering hole, if you please, and so I sent him to the Canestoga Tavern. You know where it is?"

"Yeah."

"You going to get him out of there?"

"Yeah."

"That should be fun. He was six sheets to the fucking wind."

"That's all right. So am I."

14

I was a little surprised to see the parking lot around the Canestoga Tavern jammed with cars until I remembered that it was Thursday night—payday in most of the uncivilized world—and all those potbellied beer drinkers with wire cutters hanging from their belts would be in there getting shit-faced.

How long would it be before one of them decided to make himself a local reputation by punching out a big "moom pitchur" star? If one of them hadn't already . . .

As I walked to the front door, I saw a basketball game on the television set. I didn't see anyone flying through the air. Thank God for small favors.

There were a dozen men at the bar and McCue was sitting in the middle of them. There were a dozen glasses in front of him, half of them already empty.

Everyone looked over as I came in, and when McCue saw me, he yelled, "Hey, Trace, old peckerhead, come on over and have a drink."

Somebody made room for me next to him at the bar, and I said, "Well, at least you're not in a fight. I had this vision of picking up your battered body."

"I learned a trick from Kirk Douglas that keeps me alive in strange saloons," he said.

"What's that? Snarl and grow a dimple?"

"No. I walk up and wait for everybody to recognize me and then I pound my fist on the bar and shout, 'Every man in the house can lick me.' That always seems to do the trick. Then I buy everybody a drink, and they buy me one back, and before you know it, we're all friends."

"And all drunk," I said.

"Naturally. What in hell do you think I come to a tavern for? Hey, everybody, this is my friend Trace."

Some guy with a stomach that belonged to the ages asked me, "You an actor too?"

"McCue, God bless him, answered for me. "No," he said. "Trace is my bodyguard. Toughest guy in forty states."

"Why only forty states?" the guy said, measuring me with a look that said I wasn't so tough. I'd have agreed if McCue ever shut up and gave me a chance.

McCue said, "Because we haven't been in fights in all fifty states yet."

I said, "Thanks, pal. You're on your way to getting my nose busted."

"Think nothing of it," McCue said with his best smile.

Before I could do anything about it, there were four drinks in front of me, and because I always worry about the people starving in India, I had to drink them. The bartender was the same charming fellow I'd met that afternoon. I told him no more drinks for McCue and me.

There were another dozen people sitting around at tables across the room, and occasionally one of them would pop up to the bar to buy us a drink. The bartender would nod and take their money and then follow my instructions and not pour us a drink.

The guy with the belly said to me, "You really that tough?"

The trouble with that question is that there's no answer that doesn't buy you trouble. If you say yes, you're going to be challenged. If you say no, the guy's going to think you're making fun of him and you're going to be challenged.

I sipped my drink and said. "Tony doesn't need me to do his fighting for him. He's the toughest man I ever saw." That'd teach that bastard. Let him get his own nose broken.

The bartender announced last call at five minutes to one. The room let out a collective groan.

"Sorry," he said. "Closing's at one. Those are the rules."

"You stayed open late last week when your stupid brother-in-law was here from Buffalo," one man at the bar said.

"Yeah. But I was hoping he'd choke on one of the free drinks and die. Drink up. You guys are done for tonight."

The guy with the belly went to the men's room. I didn't see him come out and I finally got McCue to his feet and told him we were leaving.

Naturally, he had to do an exit speech.

"Gentlemen," he roared, and the bar quieted down. "We want to thank you all for showing us such a good time. We'll be back again to see you all. Bring the wives and kiddies."

He left two twenty-dollar bills as a tip. They vanished into the bartender's hands with the speed of light, I guess before any of his customers could steal the cash.

Outside, I realized why I hadn't seen the guy with the belly come out of the bathroom. He was standing near the trunk of McCue's white Rolls-Royce, alongside a short wiry man whose lips sank in as if he had already taken out his false teeth in anticipation of trouble.

McCue was wobbling from side to side, lurching against me. He saw the two men standing together twenty-five feet away and staggered to a halt. "Trace, does this mean what I think it does?"

"I think it means you're going to get your ass kicked," I said.

"Surely you wouldn't let that happen to me."

"Why not?" I said.

"Damned if I know," he said. "Wait. The movie. Think of all the people who are dependent on me. If I get a broken nose, there's no movie. Oh, Trace. All those people out of work. The widows, the orphans."

"Oh, you're a pain in the ass," I said.

I took a step forward and McCue said, "Across this land, women and children will go to bed, blessing your name in their prayers. God bless you, Trace. God bless you."

"Listen," I said. "When I'm killed, I don't want anybody but you to speak over my grave. You're the best I ever saw."

"I'll sneak you right into heaven," he said, and grinned again. It was hard to be mad at a man who grinned like that.

I walked up to the Rolls-Royce and said, "What can we do for you, fellas?"

"You just back off, pal," the one with the stomach said. "I want him." He pointed past me at McCue. "I want to see if he's as tough as he looks in the movies."

"Unh-unh," I said, and shook my head.

"You going to stop me?" he said.

"Look, pal, let's not make this a talking contest. If Tony was allowed to, he'd wipe up the street with you. With both of you. But he's on a movie and he's not allowed to get his hands bloodied; it screws up the filming schedule. Now, we're going to get in the car and drive away. If you want a fight, let's get it on and get it over with, but let's not stand here, who said, you said, I said, what said, it's too goddamn cold for that. What's your pleasure, pal?"

"This." He lunged forward from the back of the car and threw a big roundhouse right hand, so slow you could have preserved it in amber. I leaned back. It missed. I leaned forward. I didn't. I buried a left hand deep into his belly, and the air came out of him. He tossed himself forward and threw both arms around me. I ducked, slipped out, backed up a step, and hit him a right hand in the side of the face. He dropped.

I turned toward the smaller guy with the bad teeth. Before I could say anything, McCue was standing alongside me. He told the smaller man, "It'll take two tougher guys than you to take us on."

Us? I thought.

"Now get your friend out of here," McCue said, "before you find out what trouble is really like."

The smaller man nodded, helped Beer Belly to his feet, and led him away.

McCue and I watched them go, then the actor clapped his hands together, and said, "Hot damn. I love bad dialogue."

"Let's just get out of here before they change their minds and come back with their seven brothers," I said. "Can you drive?"

"I can not only drive. I can sing while driving. 'I talk to the trees but them peckerheads won't listen to me.' " He was roaring unmelodiously at the top of his voice.

"I'll drive," I said. "Where are the keys?"

"In the car."

"You leave the keys to a Rolls-Royce in the car?"

"If I don't, I lose them," McCue said.

"All right." All the car's doors were open, so I kind of shoved him in the back seat and drove away from the ginmill.

Great ride. He was singing "La donna è mobile" in pig latin. I looked around. Somewhere the son of a bitch had found a bottle and was drinking from it. He wiped his mouth with the back of his hand. I looked back toward the road and he said, "The great tragedy of my life. I could have been a great operatic tenor."

"What went wrong?"

"I turned out to be a baritone."

"Right," I said. "Who wants to be a baritone? The tenors get all the songs and all the women."

"Exactly. It's always the tenors who are hoisting their glasses and raising their voices in song. Baritones don't get shit to sing," he bellowed. "They might as well hum, for all anybody cares. I couldn't stand not being noticed."

"I've observed that peculiarity," I said.

The guard at the gate was disappointed when he saw me driving, but he brightened when he saw Tony sprawled across the back seat, screaming, savaging "Di quella pira" from *Trovatore*.

"For you, my good and faithful servant," Tony said, and handed the guard the bottle.

"Thanks," the guard said as he went to open the gate.

"Don't worry, Trace, I've got more," McCue shouted into my ear.

I parked the car and left the keys in it. What the hell. I could be every bit as irresponsible as he was. Then I helped him up the steps toward the darkened Canestoga Falls Hotel.

There was a small night-light on as I helped McCue up the stairs.

He said, "Do you want me to recite 'The Face on the Barroom Floor'?"

"No."

"Okay. Then I'll sing. "Oh, you can't chop your poppa up in Massachusetts, not even if it's meant as a surprise . . .""

"Shhh," I said.

"Ooops, sorry. People sleeping, right?"

"Right. Listen, we've got to make a deal."

"I'm all ears."

"You stop trying to sneak out on me," I said. "It's a pain in the ass to have to drive around trying to find you."

"That sounds like a rotten deal to me," he said. "What do I get out of it?"

"I won't try to stop you from drinking."

"No?" he said.

"No. I don't give a rat's ass how much you drink."

"Okay," he said.

"A deal?"

"You have the word of a thespian on it."

"What's that worth?" I asked.

He stopped in the middle of the hallway, separated himself from me, and drew himself up to his full height. "Sir, I never lie. I deceive, but I never lie."

"I'll remind you of that," I said. I left him off in front of his door and went back to my own room. On the floor inside the door, I found a note.

It read: "Your father called tonight. Telephone him tomorrow. Important." It was signed "Snapp."

If it had been real important, Sarge would have said to call him tonight, so I put that out of my mind and began to undress.

As I laid my jacket and shirt over the back of a chair, I realized that Chico was unreasonable. She always said I was a slob because I hung my clothes neatly on a chair when I take them off. I think this is elegant; she thinks it's clear evidence that I am a dirtbag.

"Where *should* I put them?" I asked her once.

"In the closet, like everyone else does."

"Hah. How little you know. Only fourteen percent of American men put their clothes in the closet when they take them off at night, and all those men watch the *Phil Donahue Show*. I read that in Chapter 912 of *The Playboy Philosophy*. Nobody hangs their clothes up, Chico. Suppose they're dirty. Suppose they're sweaty. Then they dirty and sweat up all the clean clothes in your closet. Best wait till morning till you're sober, and you can make an honest evaluation of the state of your clothes. I'm surprised you didn't know that."

"What difference does it make?" she had said. "You wear them again anyway."

"That's just the way things work out sometimes. My clothes always happen to be clean because I am a very neat and orderly person."

"Your clothes are always reeking with alcohol that you spilled on yourself during the night."

"If you're going to resort to personal attack, I'm not going to discuss this with you anymore," I had said.

There are a lot of things women just don't understand. I took off my pants and neatly put them across the back of a chair. Then I took the jacket from the bed and put that on the chair and then hung the shirt over it. I took off my socks and laid them neatly across the tops of my shoes to air out.

Satisfied that I had done everything good breeding and simple hygiene required, I was standing there in my underwear when the hall door was pushed open.

Tony McCue stood in the open doorway, wavering from side to side, his famous apologetic smile on his face.

"What's the matter?"

"I seem to be having trouble opening my door,"

McCue said. "They don't make doors like they used to."

"Did you try turning the knob?" I asked.

"My first line of attack," he said. "When that didn't work, I swore. Then I kicked it. Nothing worked. It's hopeless, Trace. I'm a man without a home. Can I bunk with you?"

"No," I said. I walked past McCue and down the hall. He followed me. I turned the doorknob and pushed his door open.

"It seems to have magically corrected itself," McCue said. Suddenly he threw his hand up to his mouth. "Help me in," he said. "I think I've got to do va-va."

"Va-va?" I said.

"Quick. The bathroom," McCue said.

I grabbed his arm and steered him through the bedroom. He ran for the toilet, lowered his head over it, and threw up.

That was it, I figured. Chico might want to be a detective and carry a freaking gun, but if the work involved helping grown men throw up, it wasn't for me. Case closed.

I started for the door, then stopped. Suppose McCue decided to drown himself in the toilet bowl? I would stay, but I wouldn't watch him, though. I couldn't stand to see a grown man puke.

I saw McCue's pill bottles on the countertop of the sink. One of the bottles was on its side and pills spilled out. I remember they had been neatly stacked when I was up here earlier, looking for McCue.

He flushed the toilet, stood up, and washed out his mouth in the sink. Then he splashed cold water on his face.

"Must have been something I ate," he said. "God, I feel like shit."

"You look like it too," I said.

He brushed by me and walked back into the living room of the suite. I saw him empty the single tray of ice cubes in the freezer into a silver-colored ice bucket. He found a bottle of gin in a dresser drawer.

"I need a drink," he said.

"You need to sleep."

"I have to get a pill." He brushed by me again and went into the bathroom.

I followed him and as he picked up one of the vials of drugs, I caught his hand. "Don't take them," I said.

"Why not?"

"It's a long story. Trust me."

"I can't sleep without pills," he said.

"Tonight you will," I said.

I steered him back into the bedroom and pushed him down, fully clothed, onto the bed.

"You know we're blood brothers now, don't you?" he said. "It's like we cut our wrists and mingled our blood."

"Why?"

"An old Chinese proverb," he said. "Once you see a grown man heave, you have a responsibility for his life."

"Especially if your company is carrying an insurance policy on his life. Go to sleep."

"I'll try if you make me a drink."

"Okay." I went outside, found a glass, filled it with ice cubes, and poured a little gin on top.

"Lots of ice," he yelled from the bedroom.

I handed him the drink. He raised it to his lips, spilled most of it on his face, and passed out. I took the drink away and put it on the end table. Then I went into the bathroom and collected all his pills and took them with me. When I got back to my room, I stuck them in a dresser drawer and went to bed.

McCue was snoring well. I fell asleep to it.

Later I woke up. My luminous wristwatch said it was

almost four A.M. I never wake up in the middle of the night. Why this time?

I was listening and I heard a sound in the hallway.

That was why. That son of a bitch was trying to sneak out again. I got up and walked to the door and opened it softly. I'd trap the bastard.

But I didn't see McCue. Instead, I saw Tami Fluff, wearing a satin gown and maribou slippers standing outside his door. She opened the door and went inside.

For a moment I was annoyed that I hadn't locked McCue's door, until I remembered that I couldn't have. The door locked only from inside the room.

What the hell did Tami Fluff want?

I lay back down and got my answer. McCue's snoring stopped and Tami Fluff's sounds started. She squealed a couple of times. She let out a cry of delight. It took about twenty minutes. Then I heard McCue's snores reverberating again. A minute after that I heard soft footsteps going past my door.

Good. Now if maybe everybody was finished jiving and chucking, maybe I could get some sleep.

Good night, world.

15

The phone woke me up before I was ready to get up. I know there are some people who can ignore phones, even sleep through them, but I'm not one of them. Suppose it's the lottery office telling me I won? Suppose it's the IRS telling me that they made a mistake and they owe me fifty thousand dollars? Suppose it's my ex-wife calling to tell me that she is going to jump off the George Washington Bridge? Upper deck. Suppose it was Sarge calling back?

Unfortunately, this call wasn't any of those. It was Tony McCue, who said, "Good morning, old sport."

"What do you want?"

"I want to get up," he said.

"Here," I said. "Hoist yourself to a sitting position, then swing around on your ass until your feet are hovering over the floor, lurch forward, and you're up."

"Easy for you to say," McCue said.

"Easy to do."

"I can't get up. You took my pills, you Irish bastard. I need a pill in the morning to get my heart started."

"Fake it with the heart," I said. "Nobody will notice."

"You give me my pills or I'm calling the police," he said.

"Why do *I* have your pills?"

"You took them last night."

"Let me think," I said. I thought a long time and then I remembered taking them. Then I remembered why. "You can't have those pills," I said.

"I'll never be able to get out of bed without them."

"You'd be better able to get out of bed if you didn't spend all night screwing," I said.

"Screwing?"

"Yes. I heard you."

"Damn. I thought there was somebody here last night," he said.

"Look," I said, "I'm awake now. Why don't you get dressed and we'll go get breakfast."

"Screwing, huh? Can you tell me something?" McCue said.

"Try me."

"Was it good for her too?"

"She sounded happy," I said.

"Good. Can you tell me something else?"

"What?"

"Who was it?"

"Get dressed," I said.

As long as I had the damned telephone in my hand, I decided to call Sarge. He was at the office early. Why not? If I lived with my mother, I'd be at the office 168 hours a week.

"Tracy Investigations."

"Hi, Sarge."

"Listen, son. You asked me to check on that accident?"

"Right."

"It doesn't quite go down right," Sarge said.

"How's that?"

"The guy who got killed was just a guy. Single,

assistant credit manager at a bank, nothing to worry about."

"So?"

"But the guy who drove the car," Sarge said. "There were witnesses there, son. They said this guy ran down the other guy and then peeled off like he was on his way into orbit. But at the end of the block, he broadsided a cab and got his head smashed up. Killed instantly."

"He was hit-and-running, though?"

"Looks that way," Sarge said. "Anyway, the dead driver was this Mafia goon from around Albany. A very bad actor with a long record. And he was carrying an unlicensed gun."

"I see," I said.

"So you tell me. Why'd you want me to check out an accident and how come it just turns out that the driver is a mob guy?"

"This dead driver?" I asked. "Would he be the kind of guy who might take a contract to kill somebody? Could that explain the gun?"

"This guy was bad, son. He'd take a contract to do Godzilla if it paid enough. What's it all about?"

"The guy who got killed," I said. "He was wearing Tony McCue's white hat and coat. I just wondered if maybe that hit-and-run accident was meant for McCue."

"You might be onto something, son," Sarge said.

"I think so. Last night I think somebody was messing with McCue's pills."

Sarge was quiet for a moment. Then he said, "It's starting to look like you might have to earn that five hundred a day. Want me to come up and give you a hand?"

"Not yet, Sarge. I'll keep you posted."

"Okay. I'll tell you one thing."

"What's that?"

"I'm just glad you've got that gun I gave you," he said.

"I'll call you later," I said. I showered, and when I came out of the bathroom, McCue was sitting in my bedroom, looking through a four-year-old copy of *Reader's Digest* and looking as if he had just emerged from a health spa. He wore an open-throat red-striped shirt, white jeans, and tan buckskin shoes.

"Put on some clothes, you're disgusting," he told me.

"That's nothing compared to watching you toss your cookies into the toilet bowl," I said.

"I heaved?" he said.

"Yes."

"No wonder I didn't throw up this morning. I took care of it last night."

"Get up. You're sitting on my clothes."

I dug a clean shirt and clean socks out of the pile in the drawer and used a bottom drawer as a hamper for my dirty clothes. McCue moved over and sat on the bed as I put on the same slacks and jacket I'd worn yesterday.

He looked at me and said, "Traveling light, I see,"

"The mark of the experienced traveler," I said.

"The mark of the slob."

"Did you come here to hassle me on my wardrobe?"

"No," he said. "On my pills. Where are they?"

"See, you don't need them," I said. "You said you couldn't move in the morning without one, and here you are, snotty, well-dressed, pampered, and much too rich. And without taking a pill."

"Without a pill, my ass. I had to dip into my emergency supply. I keep them inside a hollowed-out bible."

"I don't know," I said, "but I think somebody was messing around with your medicine last night. When I was in your room early, all the containers were neat behind the faucets, but when we went back in there later, some of them were spilled out. That's why I didn't want you to take them."

McCue was pensive. "No great problem," he said finally. "I'll have Doctor Death run into town and get me fresh prescriptions. She owes that to me for making love to her last night."

"It wasn't Ramona," I said.

"Oh, my God. Who was it?"

"Dahlia Codwell," I said.

He shook his head. "I've really got to start watching my drinking."

We walked downstairs, and on the first-floor landing he touched my arm. "Trace?"

"What?"

"Why would somebody mess with my pills?"

"I don't know, but I'm beginning to get a hunch that maybe somebody's trying to kill you. You have any enemies?"

"Everyone here. All of them."

"Maybe one of them hates you worse than all the others," I said.

"Well, that isn't nice," he said with a voice slow and deep with sorrow. "I'm turning over a new leaf, Trace. From now on, I'm going to be nice to everybody. Everybody."

16

As resolutions go, it was a good resolution, and as resolutions go, it went, because the first thing McCue did when he walked into the dining room was to pose in the open doorway, shout "Good morning, you murderous bastards," and then walk up to Arden Harden, who was sitting alone at a table and say, "Well, well, well. If it isn't the Jolly Green Midget."

Harden refused to look up. Last night, when he dressed like a human, he had looked like Mel Tormé gone sour with his little F U sweater. Today he looked like a break dancer out on parole. He was wearing a one-piece red satin jumpsuit, but it was cut like a jet pilot's uniform with zippered pockets running every which way.

McCue said, "Mind if we join you?"

"Yes," Harden said.

"Thank you. That's very gracious," McCue said. We sat down and McCue poured us both coffee from the large stainless-steel pitcher already on the table. Also on the table was an open paper bag that looked as if it held birdseed.

McCue looked around the room. Dahlia Codwell was sitting with the Scotts and Roddy Quine. Mrs. Scott seemed to have gotten into the Hollywood swing of things because she was wearing makeup that looked like it belonged on stage at the Folies Bergère and black wraparound sunglasses. McCue favored Dahlia Codwell with a big wave and a warm grin. She gave him the finger.

"There's your answer," he whispered to me. "It wasn't good for her either."

For a moment I didn't know what he was talking about. Then I remembered telling him he had taken Codwell to bed last night. He must have believed it.

I looked for Tami Fluff. She was at another table with Ramona, Birnbaum, and Sheila Hallowitz. Everybody was chatting merrily.

I lit a cigarette and remembered I had to get more today.

Harden looked up from his cereal bowl and said, "Are you really going to smoke at the table? It makes me sick."

"It makes us sick to see people eating unwrapped Mouse Knots," McCue said.

I told McCue, "Nice, nice. Remember. Be nice."

"Oops. Right. You're really looking fine today, Arden," he said. "I really love your suit. Did Diana Ross mind selling it to you?"

"Another thing," Harden said. "How am I supposed to get any work done if you're going to be parading up and down the hall all night, you and your gang of visitors?"

"Simple answer to that," McCue said mildly. "Don't work. We don't. Why should you be any different?"

"Wait a minute," I said. "What visitors?"

"Who knows?" Harden said. "Did you know, Tracy, that actors have the lowest IQs of anybody smarter than a garden snail? There's a special category for actors, halfway between moron and imbecile."

"Yes. They call it rich man's land," McCue said. "Don't be bitter. You may still have a growth spurt. Trace, I need breakfast. You too?"

"Yes."

"What'll you have?" he asked me.

"What've they got, do you think?"

"Vodka and gin."

"I'll have vodka," I said.

"You two are disgusting," Harden said. When McCue walked to the bar, he said to me, "I thought you might be able to civilize him while you were here, but you're just as bad as he is."

"I'm sorry about the disturbances last night," I said, trying to sound sincere. "You were in your room working?"

"Yes. I work all the time. And I need peace and quiet."

"You didn't see who went to McCue's room?"

"No. A lot of people. All night long."

"But you didn't look out, maybe, to see who they were?"

"No. Why should I?"

"And you were in your room all night?"

"Of course. If I left, some idiot might come up and start messing with my script. I couldn't have that. The goddamn doors don't even have locks on them. I hate this place. My room's too small. And too cold. I slept with towels on top of my blankets last night."

McCue came back with two glasses stuffed with ice and liquor. He set them on the table, then walked past me to the table where Birnbaum was sitting with Sheila, Tami Fluff, and the doctor. McCue tapped Ramona on the shoulder and the two of them walked a few steps away from the table. McCue was talking earnestly; Ra-

mona looked annoyed. The actor shrugged and returned
to our table. Harden stood up and folded his paper bag
tightly. From under the table, he took a leather over-
night bag, put the paper bag inside, and zipped it up. I
could see the leather bag held a pile of yellow legal-size
pads.

He said nothing to us but turned to the door.

Then Dahlia Codwell called out his name, "Arden."

He turned and she motioned him to come sit alongside her. I didn't know; maybe she was going to tell him
how little he knew about the movie business.

What I was thinking about was what kind of staff the
hotel had. Except for Clyde Snapp, the old guy I'd met
at the gate, and the uniformed cretin on guard duty last
night, I hadn't seen anyone. But last night, there had
been steak and eggs and fish and four different kinds of
vegetables for dinner, and today there were large stain-
less chafing dishes filled with eggs, pancakes, sausage,
bacon, and Danish pastries. I never saw a cook or a
waiter or a busboy. I never saw anyone take away the
dirty dishes. I never saw anyone on the front desk.
Whoever was running this place should be hired by the
Pentagon, I thought, because this was real efficiency.
And I hoped they were efficient enough to have a
cigarette machine on the premises because I had only
one left and then it was gone because McCue took it and
lighted it.

He and I were the only smokers. I used to wonder
why drinkers smoked so much until a doctor cleared up
the mystery for me. This doctor told me that the body
was a perfect biofeedback machine and it tried all the
time to keep the body itself in perfect equilibrium.

Now, when you drank, your blood vessels dilated
and got larger, which the body didn't like; it wanted
them normal. So messages passed back and forth between the glands and the brain, and suddenly the body

told you it wanted a cigarette. Taste had nothing to do with it. The body wanted nicotine because nicotine helped close down those dilated blood vessels. It was all part of the body's way of maintaining equilibrium.

"Is that really true?" I asked the doctor.

"Damned if I know. But you've got to admit, it is one marvelously elegant theory," he said.

That it was. But the truth might be a more common stone. I think sometimes that people who drink a lot do it because they're social misfits. And social misfits who get out in public never know what to do with their hands, so they fill them with cigarettes. That's elegant too.

Biff Birnbaum came over to the table and said to McCue, "Roddy and I are going out to look at the grounds, to see where we're going to shoot some of the stuff. Come on out with us."

"Must I?" McCue said.

"Only if you want to get paid," Birnbaum said.

"Why don't we go out and look at the grounds to see where we're going to shoot some of the stuff?" McCue said.

"Good idea," Birnbaum said. "Whenever you're ready."

"I'm ready now. Can Trace come?"

Birnbaum looked pained. "Actually, Roddy would rather he didn't."

"Why's that?" McCue asked.

"He thinks, well, Tracy's a civilian, he'll ask a lot of stupid questions."

"He couldn't ask them of a more likely person," McCue said.

"That's all right, Tony," I said. "I have to get cigarettes anyway."

"If you have to go out, try to hold off till I come back. That way we can ransom your car."

Birnbaum said, "Let me get my jacket. I'll be right

back." He was already wearing his New York Mets jacket. Maybe, I thought, he put another jacket over it when he went outdoors.

After he left the table, McCue said, "Are you sure I screwed Dahlia last night? She didn't seem real warm to me today."

"It sounded like her," I said. "I could be wrong." For some reason, I didn't want to tell him I had lied to him. It had seemed funny at the time, but it didn't seem so funny now.

Later Ramona Dedley came to my table and sat across from me. She was wearing very short shorts that threatened the hotel's PG rating and a scoop-necked blouse that really scooped.

" 'Morning, Doctor."

"Did Tony sleep with that little tramp last night?"

"Which little tramp?" I said.

"Fluff. Did Tony sleep with her?"

Sleep with? I loved people who used euphemisms because it always gives the dedicated professional the chance to mislead without actually technically lying. I learned that early. Sarge had sent me to a Jesuit college—I think largely to bust my Jewish mother's chops—and one day I was waiting to see the dean when the dean's secretary, also a priest, got a telephone call. "No," the secretary said. "The dean's not here." When he hung up, he must have seen me looking at him quizzically. He smiled and asked me, "Is he here? No, he's not. I don't see him. You don't see him, do you? He didn't ask me if the dean was in his office. He asked me if the dean was here. The dean's not here. He's in his office and you can go in and see him now."

When I came out, the priest secretary said to me, "It's called a mental reservation. Hang on to it, a very useful technique."

"I'll keep it in mind the next time I go to confession," I said.

He shook his head. "It doesn't work on God," he said. "Only on people. When you use a mental reservation on God, it counts as a lie."

"Sleep with" her?

"You're not God, are you? " I asked Ramona.

"I beg your pardon."

"Never mind. I don't think Tony slept with her. Why?"

"She was dropping hints about it at the table," Ramona said.

"Why would she do that? She doesn't even like Tony."

"Hollywood," Ramona said. "Who knows? What was Tony telling me that you took his pills?"

"Yeah. I had an idea that somebody might have been tampering with them last night."

"What gave you that idea?" she asked.

"When we came in last night, the pills had been moved. Some of them were spilled out."

"Sounds like Tony to me. He's always spilling things, knocking them over."

"He wasn't there when it happened," I said. "He was with me."

"Who, then?" she asked.

"I don't know."

"Why?"

"I don't know that either," I said. "Could you look at the pills and tell if something had been done to them?"

"I don't know. Maybe," Ramona said.

"I'll drop them at your room, but I don't think Tony ought to take any of them. Let him get new ones. He can afford them. He takes too many pills anyway."

"Is that meant to be critical, Trace?" the woman asked. I had hit a nerve because she was bristling.

"No, ma'am. You're the doctor, he's the patient, and I'm nobody. I just think any pills are too many pills."

"You're one of those hardy types? Never sick. Never take medicine. Never see a doctor."

"Something like that."

"Well, Tony's not. He has low blood sugar. He has a kidney disfunction. He's had a heart attack. He has thyroid problems. The pills . . . Dammit, you call them that but I don't. Pills make them sound like recreational drugs. There's no recreation here. The medication I prescribe for Tony is exactly what he needs, no matter how much bullshit he shovels at you. Pills? He takes Digoxin, 125 milligrams, orally, once a day. He takes . . . Oh, the hell with it. He takes what I tell him to take, when I tell him to take it." Her voice was chilly and brisk. "And I don't like being called Doctor Death."

"Maybe somebody's trying to change his prescription, Doctor," I said.

"What?"

"To poison," I said. "I'll drop those pills off at your room."

17

The kitchen was one flight down, on the basement level. I found Clyde Snapp scrubbing up dishes at a large deep sink that looked as if it had been made of poured concrete. His sleeves were rolled up, showing his knotty muscled forearms.

He heard me come in before I could speak, turned around, nodded, picked up a towel, and dried his hands. "Mr. Tracy," he said.

"Call me Trace."

He grinned. "You're not looking so bad for somebody who had such a late night."

"I hope we didn't wake you up coming in," I said.

He shook his head. "Np." I knew already that that meant "no." "I'm awake most of the time," he said. "Besides, your father called late."

"Do you have any cigarettes around here?" I asked.

"Sure. What do you smoke?"

"Anything with a filter. The milder the better."

"Let's see what we got," he said. "There's fresh coffee there on the stove if you want some."

I poured a cup as Snapp opened a cupboard that was

filled with cartons of cigarettes. "I've got Carltons," he said.

"Good. I need three or four packs." I reached in my pocket for cash, but he waved it away.

"Forget it. I'll put it on Hollywood's bill," he said. "If you need any more, they're in here and the cupboard's never locked."

I thanked him and looked around the kitchen. There was a cot against the wall in a corner. The kitchen looked as if it had been scrubbed with toothbrushes by a Marine Corps punishment detail. Everything sparkled.

"I've been in operating rooms that weren't this clean," I said admiringly. Actually, almost any room that I spent any time in wasn't that clean.

"I like things snappy clean," he said. "When things are in the right place, it makes life easier, lets you get things done."

"You the only person working here?" I asked.

"Aaaay-p."

"You're doing the cooking and cleaning and everything else?"

"Aaaay-p. Everything except standing guard at the gate. I hired some local fellers to do that, just to keep out anybody who don't belong here. That's how I knew you was late getting in last night. You and that McCue."

"Well, you're doing a hell of a job. I don't know what you're getting paid, but it isn't enough."

"It's enough," Snapp said.

"You been working here long?"

"Since the hotel closed down, about five years ago."

"Are they going to reopen it?"

"I think so. I think the owner wants to get some free publicity with this movie, so he rented the place cheap. Then, when the movie's out, he's going to reopen it."

"Who's the owner?" I said.

"Private owner. Not one of them hotel chains," he said.

"Sounds like everybody's making out but you," I said.

"How do you figure that?"

"The owner's getting publicity for the hotel. The movie people are getting low rent. Everybody's making a score except you."

"I'm getting my paycheck. Long as I get that, I figure I'm doing all right. Working hard now makes up for a lot of times when I just hung around and watched my toenails grow." He went back to the sink and started to load clean dishes into a cupboard.

I looked around again. I was drinking my coffee, leaning against a long stainless-steel table. In the wall behind me was a dumbwaiter door. There were two more spaced fifteen feet apart along the wall. Idly I opened the door behind me. There was a big pulley with a thick rope looped through it. Clumps of dust hung from the rope. A contraption that looked like a metal wedge was jammed into the pulley, sort of like a large doorstop, to prevent the cable from moving.

"I ain't been using that," Snapp said.

"No. I can tell. Would it work?"

"Sure," he said. "When the place opens up again, I'll fix them up and clean them up. It's a nice little touch, being able to send food up to the rooms that way. I get a kitchen crew in here and they can do it. Meantime, I shut them all off in the rooms upstairs, so nobody falls down the shaft."

I closed the dumbwaiter door and finished my coffee.

"The other half of the hotel that's sealed off," I said. "What's going on there?"

"I didn't get a chance to redo those rooms, paint and wallpaper and stuff. Just as well, because that's where they're going to shoot the movie. I guess for their cameras and all, they've got to tear down walls and things. Promised that when they're done they'll fix it all up. If you can trust their promises."

"Well, so far so good," I said.

He closed the dish cupboard. "They don't like to pay their rent. The first check was late, I'm told."

I heard someone running down the steps from the first floor.

Sheila Hallowitz stuck her head in the door. "Mr. Snapp. You have a first-aid kit?"

"Aaaay-p. What happened?" Snapp said. He grabbed a toolbox with a red cross pasted on top of it from under the sink.

"There's been an accident," Sheila said. "Hurry."

18

For about a hundred yards or so behind the hotel, the ground fell away toward the banks of the lake. Much of the land was clustered with trees, but there were broad paths leading through those areas. Closer to the lake, the land cleared into tightly trimmed lawn that rolled down to the water's edge and the old wooden dock.

Sheila ran fast, which made me sure she was from New York because speed is a survival skill for women there. She led us into a small clearing. A body lay on the ground.

It wasn't Tony McCue.

It was Roddy Quine. He was sprawled on his back at the base of a large rock formation. His right pants leg was rolled up and blood was oozing out of a large gash in his leg. There was a big rock, maybe fifteen inches across, on the ground alongside him.

Clyde Snapp ran up and knelt alongside him. Sheila took up her post alongside Biff Birnbaum. I saw Tony McCue leaning against a boulder on the far side of the clearing, looking bored.

"Ain't broke," Clyde said, looking up at no one in particular.

Sheila was rubbing her hands together, as if washing them of dirt.

"Pretty good gash, though," Clyde said.

"Did anyone think to call Dr. Dedley?" I asked.

"No," Birnbaum said. "Good idea, Tracy. Sheila, go get the doctor."

Sheila nodded and ran off again. She might have a career running.

"It's not broken?" Quine said to Snapp in disbelief.

"Np. If it was, you'd be screaming instead of whining," Snapp said.

"It feels broken."

"That's cause you ain't never had a leg broken," Snapp said. He took a brown plastic bottle from the first-aid kit and poured some of the liquid from it on Quine's sickly pale leg. It fizzed into a white foam.

I walked over to McCue. "What happened?" I asked him.

"The four of us were out here looking around. We were talking about one of the scenes that's going to be shot here. The hero—that's me—is chasing a killer from the house, and the killer gets to the top of the rock there and jumps off. I jump off after him. Or at least the stuntman does. I'm not jumping for this movie. So we were looking up from down here and then that rock there by Horseface came crashing down. I just happened to be turning around and I sort of saw it coming down and I pushed the two guys out of the way and jumped back. But it grazed Quine's leg."

"Quite the hero, aren't you?" I said. "You'll get the Congressional Medal of Honor for this."

"Not if anybody in Hollywood finds out who I saved. Hey. You think we can get Hard-on to come back out here and stand under that rock? If you can do that, I'll volunteer to carry the small rock back up top again. Toss it off right on his empty head."

"Were you right under the rock when it fell?" I asked.

"Pretty much, I guess. If I hadn't been looking up and seen it, it might have hit *me* on my empty head. God, I need a drink."

Snapp was closing up his First-aid kit. He told Quine, "You can get up now."

I walked past them and clambered up to alongside the rock face until I got to the ledge, ten feet above them.

I heard Quine say, "I still think it's broken."

"No. 'Tain't broke," Snapp said. "Ought to wash it off, though, and put a bandage on it, I guess." He walked back toward the path to the house and I looked around the rock ledge, although I'm no detective and I don't know what I was looking for.

All I saw was a flat ledge of rock, maybe an eight-foot square roughly. No footprints, no telltale cigarette butts, no lingering aroma of expensive French perfume, by God, and therefore the killer is . . .

I came back down as Ramona Dedley walked into the clearing. She must have been cold because she was still wearing her abbreviated breakfast costume and hadn't put on a jacket. As I came back into the clearing, she knelt over Quine and quickly confirmed Snapp's diagnosis. "It's not broken," she said. "It's not as bad as it looks either. I don't even think you'll need stitches."

"I think it's broken," Quine said. "Damn this barbarian frontier country anyway."

"Easy on the anti-American crap," McCue said.

Ramona put a bandage on the leg and fastened it with adhesive-tape strips. "You can get up," she said.

"If you say so." Quine got slowly to his feet. He stood there, swaying for a moment, as if afraid to put any weight on his injured leg.

Finally he chanced it and stood upright, evenly balanced. "I guess it's not broken," he said. He looked over at McCue. "Well, thanks, old cock. You know what the Chinese say: when you save a man's life, it belongs to you."

"No, thanks," McCue said, and started walking back to the hotel.

19

Arden Harden found us in the main dining room of the hotel. "What happened?" he asked.

"A rock fell," I said, "hit Quine, and hurt his leg."

"Were you there?" Harden asked McCue.

"Yes."

"Too bad it didn't hit you."

"You are really becoming unbearable, you malnourished twit," McCue said. "I think I'm going to drown you in the lake."

He stood up from his seat and Harden moved away to stand behind me. "You lay a hand on me and the Screenwriters Guild will have your ass. We'll close down this picture."

"Fuck it," McCue said. "Sometimes we have to sacrifice personal profit for the common good. I'm going to drown you, you bastard."

Harden ran as McCue took a step toward him. In the dining-room doorway, he turned and yelled back across the room. "You'll get yours, McCue. I'm telling you, you'll get yours."

McCue waved his arms and shouted "Boo!" and

Harden ran. The actor sat back on the stool next to me. "Even accounting for the fact that he's a midget and I'm tall and he's a nerd and I'm among the most charming of people, I don't understand why that man hates me so."

"Maybe he doesn't like what you're doing with his screenplay," I said.

"That's nonsense. Writers get their screenplays changed all the time. And what the hell do I have to do with changing his script anyway? Those two morons will do that."

"Be more specific in your reference to morons around here," I said.

"Birnbaum and Quine. They know they've got a bomb, so they're going to try to fix it."

"I guess it needs it," I said. I didn't understand films and I didn't really want to. I guess the movie generation was the one after mine.

"Except that they can't fix it," McCue said. "It'll take a real writer to fix it. One writer with one clean idea. A good movie always takes that: the clean idea. And these chowderheads never realize it. No matter how long they hang around, they never understand. So Birnbaum is going to rewrite one scene and Quine will rewrite another scene and maybe they'll even make the scenes better, but they'll make the movie worse because it won't have one clean idea running through it. Goddammit, Trace, I hate committees."

"You make this movie sound so grim that if I were you, I'd get out of it. Somehow, anyhow."

"I can't get out of it. I'm stuck by contract."

"Won't this hurt your career?"

"No. Everybody's allowed a bomb once in a while. Even Spielberg and Lucas did some disasters. And on this one, I'll just spread the word that I got forced into doing it and I think it sucks. My loyal fans will stay away in droves."

He turned around and looked out the window over the early-autumn green. The lake shimmered, slatelike, far away.

"Except for that hateful midget, it's peaceful here, isn't it?" McCue said.

"Yeah," I said. "I hate peaceful."

"Well, don't worry about it. It won't last. Nobody knows we're here yet. But when the whole cast and crew arrives on Monday, the goddamn press vultures will be following them too. They'll be up your ass and hiding under your bed and bribing people to tell them what you had for dinner and who you're screwing and who hates who, and it'll turn out to be a zoo. Do you know that two of those ditzy newspapers have somebody assigned to follow me around on a regular basis?"

"Aaaah, you love it," I said.

McCue gave me his grin. "Yeah. Ain't adulation wonderful? Let's go get your car before one of those rednecks eats it. I could use a drink too."

"You've got a drink," I said.

"A drink in a place where you're staying isn't like a drink in some neighborhood ginmill," he said. "It doesn't compare."

I told him to wait for me and went upstairs to get the drug bottles from my dresser.

Ramona Dedley was on the floor below mine directly beneath my room. As I started to knock on her door, I heard her voice inside, loud and angry.

"I know what you're up to, but I won't let you do it to him. You stop right now."

I think there was an answer, but it was soft and muffled and I couldn't understand it. I knocked and Ramona opened the door, only about a foot, and peered out through the opening.

"Oh, Trace."

"I've brought you those pills," I said, and showed her my hand.

She pointed to the dresser just inside the door. "Would you just put them there, please? I'm sorry I can't invite you in. I'm not dressed."

"That's all right," I said, and reached in to put the bottles on top of the dresser. "Is Quine all right?" I asked.

"He's fine. Carried on like he was having his leg amputated, but it was really just a nasty scratch. You'll excuse me?"

"Sure."

She closed the door and I waited a few seconds but heard no further voice from inside, so I walked downstairs and collected McCue, who was waiting impatiently for me at the front door.

McCue wanted to drive and I got in the passenger's side, but as we backed out of the spot, I saw Clyde Snapp standing by the front entrance, beckoning to me.

"Hold on just a minute," I told McCue. I got out and walked back up the stairs to where Snapp was standing. "What's up, Clyde?"

"I just thought you ought to know that that wasn't any accident before with the rock."

"What do you mean?"

"Son, I been on this property since I was a boy. That stone's been up on top of that shelf since then. It's been there through hurricane and tornado, summer and winter, at least sixty years that I know of. It didn't just suddenly fall off by its own self."

"You think somebody pushed it off?" I said.

He shook his head. "I don't know anything about that. All I know is that it didn't fall natural." He nodded once for emphasis, then turned and went back inside the hotel.

*   *   *

We parked in front of the Canestoga Tavern. Again, the parking lot was filled with cars.

McCue said, "I'll buy."

"Fine. But no fighting today."

"Not a chance," McCue said. "No one will even recognize me." He put on a pair of dark wraparound sunglasses.

"Your own mother wouldn't know you," I said.

"It always works. And we'll act like farmers."

"How do farmers act?" I asked.

"Count your change. Farmers always count their change at a bar. I tell you, Trace, they'll never know it's us."

He led the way cockily through the front door of the tavern. The room was packed, not just with men but with women and children too.

"Here he is, folks," somebody yelled. "Hooray for Tony McCue."

Everybody cheered, except me. I groaned.

McCue leaned over and whispered, "Fucking sunglasses fail again. Next time I wear the Polack baseball cap. It lowers the IQ sixty points and no one ever recognizes you."

He waved to the crowd and took off the sunglasses. We went to a small table for two in the corner of the barroom. Without being asked, the bartender brought us two drinks, McCue's packed with ice as usual. The bartender was smiling. I guess he had had a chance to count last night's receipts.

Everyone wanted an autograph. McCue, I noticed, was unfailingly polite and charming to everyone who approached. Being good-humored all the time, I thought, was a hell of a price to have to pay for being a star. That was just theoretical. Nobody asked for my autograph.

Finally, the crowd thinned out. I saw no sign of those

two rednecks that had waited for us in the parking lot the night before.

McCue said, "At last. Peace and quiet. Post time."

"I was talking to Ramona this morning," I said.

"Ignore Doctor Death," he said airily, waving a hand in dismissal. "She's always dooming and glooming."

"Maybe so, but she didn't think all this drinking was good for you."

"Shows how little she knows," McCue said. "Drinking's the best thing I do."

"It's the safest, anyway," I said.

"Certainly."

"Safer than having rocks thrown at your head," I said.

"What are you talking about?" he asked.

"Clyde Snapp said there was no way that rock just fell on its own," I said.

"You think somebody pushed it over the edge?" he asked.

"Looks that way."

"What makes you think it was meant for me?"

"Who else?"

McCue wiped his mouth on the back of his jacket sleeve. "Roddy Quine," he said. "A gift from the movie lovers of the world."

"He's harmless. Nobody would try to kill him."

"All right. Maybe somebody trying to get rid of Birnbaum," McCue said.

"Why?" I asked. "Who?"

"Anybody who knows him. Maybe even his mother for changing his name from Irving to Barf."

"Maybe," I said. "Except I doubt if anybody was messing around last night with *his* pills."

"He doesn't take pills," McCue said. "He eats weights for breakfast." He finished his drink and said, "You really think somebody was messing with my pills?"

"One of the bottles was knocked over. You didn't do it and I didn't do it. Anyway, I gave them to Ramona. She's going to try to get them analyzed."

"Well, this is one hell of a pile of crap," McCue said. "Somebody trying to kill me."

"I just want you to be wary. And talk to Ramona tonight."

"Anything special?"

"Find out who was in her room today. Just before we left."

"How am I going to do that?"

"Your characters always figure out things like that," I said. "Where's your inventiveness?"

"In some scriptwriter's head," McCue said.

"All right. Tell her at three o'clock you went up to her room and you were going to knock but you heard her talking to someone. So you didn't want to disturb her. Who was she talking to?"

"Okay. What does it matter, though, who it was?"

"She was yelling at someone. I thought it might have something to do with today's accident," I said. "Just find out."

"Consider it done. But I think you're making too much of nothing," he said.

"Maybe, but you think about this. Today a rock almost got you. Last night someone was messing with your pills. And that hit-and-run accident back in the city? That guy was wearing your clothes and got run-down by somebody who may have been a professional hit man. And just maybe he thought it was you. We're taking no chances."

He made no more protests.

20

McCue drove off in the Rolls-Royce, but I walked across the street to the small general store before going back to the hotel.

Some heavy dark clouds were rolling in over the lake, and the smell of an approaching thunderstorm was in the air. The same dumb guard was working the gate and now that he knew I wasn't a movie star, he just waved me through without bothering to leave the security booth.

I heard people in the dining room and went down the stairs alongside the unoccupied registration desk and found Clyde Snapp lying on the cot in the corner of the kitchen.

"Banker's hours again, huh?" I said.

"Np. Finished cooking dinner. Nothing to do for a while till cleanup time."

"I've been thinking about what you said."

"No accident, you mean?"

"Right. You sure of that?" I asked.

"Sure as death," Snapp said. He raised himself to a

sitting position on the couch. "Don't like to talk to somebody lying down," he said. "Be dead soon enough."

"How can you be sure?" I said.

"Well, I told you. I been here a long time and I know every piece of this property. When you put a small rock on top of a big flat rock and it stays there sixty years without falling, well, it don't just fall by itself all of a sudden."

"There's always a first time."

"A first time for somebody to push it," Snapp said.

"Maybe you're right. Have you seen the owner of this place sulking around by any chance?" I said.

"No. Why?"

"Well, I thought maybe he's pissed off at slow checks from the movie guys. Maybe he decides he wants them out of here. Maybe he figures a high-class death on his hotel grounds will make the place a big tourist attraction."

Snapp grinned slowly. "I don't think he's ever thought of that, but count on it, I'm going to tell him. Maybe I'll get a raise for being so brainy."

"Who is the owner anyway?" I asked.

"My orders are not to tell anybody. He don't like his name booted around. Hey, I forgot. You got a phone call while you was out."

"Walter Marks, right?"

"Yeah. Sounded like that. Nasty-sounding fella."

"That's him. Did he say what he wanted?"

"Just for you to call."

"Okay. Anyway, reason I came down." I fished in my pocket and handed Snapp what I'd bought at the general store.

"A padlock. What's that for?"

"I want you to put it on the door of McCue's room."

"Why him? Rock didn't hit him. It hit that Englishman."

"Yeah, but I'm not paid to protect the Englishman. Just McCue. I don't want to take any chances."

"You think that rock was meant for him?"

"Got me," Trace said. "Can you put that lock on tonight?"

Snapp got up from the cot. "Sure. Do it right now. I'll need a key, though. Just for security, in case there's a fire or something."

"I had an extra made," I said, and handed it to him. "I've got two others, one for me and one for him."

"You think of everything, son."

"Then how come I don't know what I'm doing?" I said.

"Don't know as how I believe that," he said.

"Believe it," I said.

21

"Hello, Walter, old buddy. Ho, ho, ho."

"I hate it when you call me at home," Marks said. "I was just having dinner."

"Supermarket have a special on houseflies?"

"Please. No insults. What is it you wanted?"

"How quickly they forget," I said. "Remember? You called me. Ho, ho, ho."

"Of course I remember. I just wanted to know how things were going up there with the Six-million-dollar Man. And stop that ho, ho, ho."

I had to think for a moment. If I told Marks everything was sweetness and light, he might pull me off the case and there went five hundred dollars a day. But if I told him that somebody was trying to kill Tony McCue, he might send up a team of bodyguards, and again, I'd be off the case. It was a quandary, so I decided to do what I do best: I lied.

"It's real tough," I said. "McCue's a madman. I had to pull him off the roof last night. Today he wanted to go waterskiing in this frozen lake. I'm not getting a moment's rest, nursemaiding this idiot. Walter, I want to come home. Have somebody else do this."

"Not a chance, Trace," Marks said, as I knew he would.

"Come on, Walter. I'd rather go visit my ex-wife and her kids than be with this maniac. He's going to get me killed if I'm not careful."

"That's the trouble with you, Trace. You're always too cautious. Take some chances with your life. Die."

"I don't think my life and death is a subject for levity, Walter," I said.

"This isn't levity. All I want is for you to keep that McCue alive. No jerking around, Trace. Is he a terrible boozehound?"

"Worse than me."

"The man obviously ought to be committed," Marks said.

"Really, Walter, it's dangerous here for me. I really want to come home. Find somebody else to do this. I'm pleading with you."

"No. Absolutely not. I'm sorry that McCue is causing you trouble, but that's why we're paying you five hundred dollars a day to deal with that kind of trouble. It's your job, and that's final."

"Got to go now, Walter," I said hurriedly.

"What's the matter?"

"I'm looking out the window and that freaking McCue is climbing an electric pole."

"What's he doing that for?"

"I don't know. At lunch I heard him tell somebody that you can hang from electric wires and not get electrocuted as long as your feet aren't touching the ground. He's probably trying to prove it."

"Go get him. Go get him. Go get him," Marks screamed.

"See you, Groucho. Got to go. Ho, ho, ho."

I pressed down the receiver button. While I waited for another dial tone, I heard a tapping sound. It was coming from next door and I realized, after a moment, that it was probably Arden Harden typing. I dialed another number.

"Hello, Chico."

"Bastard."

"How do you do? And I am Cyrano de Bergerac at your service."

"Don't get smart with me," Chico said.

"Are you going to tell me what's wrong or do I have to guess?" I asked.

"I was talking to Sarge. He told me your gun permit arrived."

"That's right," I said. "I don't know why that upsets you. I'm not going to shoot *you*!"

"Where's mine?"

"Damned if I know," I lied. "Probably someplace in the bureaucracy or the post office. You know how things are."

"This is how I know how things are. It probably came and you probably hid it and you are probably lying to me about it, because you don't want me to have a gun."

This was indisputably, absolutely correct, I realized. I was astonished, as usual, at how accurate Chico always was in guessing my behavior. "That is a total unmitigated cruel lie," I said. "I want you to have a gun. I live for the day when you'll have a gun."

"You may live just *until* the day when I have a gun." she said.

"Threats will not deter me from doing what I know is right," I said. "I will defend to the death your right to bear arms. The Constitution of the United States says that. It doesn't talk about Japanese-Sicilians specifically, but I'm sure you're covered. I bet you could even join a militia if you wanted. You want to join a militia?"

"Trace, you'd better not be jerking me around with my gun permit. Are you carrying a gun?"

"No."

"Why not?"

"Sarge gave me his old gun, but it was so heavy I needed a wheelbarrow to carry it around. I didn't think I'd be able to carry out secret surveillances pushing a wheelbarrow."

"You're not messing around with my gun permit?" she said.

"No. Honestly I am not."

"All right," she said. "We'll let it slide for now. What's going on?"

"I think somebody might be trying to kill Tony McCue."

"Really?"

"Yes." I told her about the hit-and-run accident, the pills being shifted around in his room, and then about the falling rock out behind the hotel.

"It could just be coincidences," she said.

"Could be. Anyway, I'm here for the duration, so I've got to deal with it."

"Save his life, you'll be a big hero," she said. "It'll make our firm famous. Especially if you catch the would-be killer. Have you told Walter Marks?"

"No."

"Why not? Maybe he'd send you help."

"You don't understand him as well as I do. We need this work, so I just told him McCue was a pain in the ass and needed a nursemaid and I didn't want to be a nursemaid, so naturally Groucho ordered me to stay on the job. We have to protect our fee."

"You have such a duplicitous turn of mind," Chico

said, "that again I suspect you're jerking around with my gun permit."

"I am not. I'm sure it'll be there waiting for you when you get to New York. Are you ever getting to New York?"

"Soon now. I'm packing and I've leased this place for a year with an option if both parties agree."

"Who'd you rent to?"

"Some guy from New Jersey who owns a restaurant. He's kind of retiring."

"Don't give him a key until you're sure his check clears the bank. I know something about restaurant owners from New Jersey."

"The check was certified," she said.

"All right. I still don't trust him, though. I want you to finish my inventory, just in case he tries to steal something."

"That's a laugh," Chico said. "Finish *your* inventory."

"What do you mean, a laugh? I started one and left it on the kitchen table," I said.

"Yes. I have it right here. It has two words on it. 'Furniture' and 'dishes.' Was this what you consider an inventory of household property?"

"It was a start, wasn't it?"

"Forget it. I'll do one. Any women coming on to you?"

"No. They all hate me."

"Amazing. And they haven't even had the benefit of speaking with me."

"Get to New York rapidly, will you please? I miss you."

"Same here, although I never understand why."

"Because you know that someday I'm going to be rich and powerful and you want to be on my good side when I start to crush the little people," I said.

"Yes. You can club them over the head with your household inventory," she said.

"Did you give notice at the casino?"

"Yes. I'm done 'cause my vacation time covers my notice. The other blackjack dealers are giving me a party."

"When? Where?"

"Tonight. Here," she said.

"I don't trust dealers. Make them sign the inventory too," I said.

When I finished with Chico, I called my father. H· was in the office late.

"Tracy Investigations."

"Sarge, this is your wandering son."

"Hi, champ. How goes it in Lotusland East? You bang any movie stars yet?"

"You know I've given that stuff up," I said.

"Yeah. I talked to Chico today."

"I know you did," I said. "Listen, Sarge, something slipped my mind."

"What was that?"

"Remember the other day when Chico's gun permit arrived."

"Yeah. I didn't tell her about it," he said.

"I know. Well, somehow the permit wound up under the left cushion on the couch."

"*Somehow* it wound up there."

"Yes. It's a long story. Anyway, somehow it wound up there. So what I want you to do is take it out, and then, whenever you talk to Chico, tell her it just arrived in the mail. You got it? It *just* arrived in the mail."

"I've got it. Hold on," Sarge said.

He set the phone down. A moment later, he said, "It's there. The gun I gave you is there too."

"Yeah. Somehow that got stuck under the cushion too," I said.

"You're up there, among all those ferocious Hollywood types, without a gun?"

"Of course. I always try charm first before I shoot anybody," I said.

"I'll tell Chico it just arrived when she calls. And I'll hold the gun. You'll change your mind. How's it going, by the way?"

I told him about the latest episode with the falling rock.

"Starting to sound like a pattern, isn't it?" he said.

"Yeah. But it could still just be coincidences," I said.

"Yeah. And it could snow in July, but don't bet on it."

"I won't," I said. "Listen. If you talk to Groucho, don't mention any of this to him."

"Okay. Mother wants to know when you're coming for dinner again."

"When Halley's comet returns," I said.

"I'll tell her," he said dryly. "She likes having specific dates."

22

Harden was still tapping away when I walked downstairs to the dining room. The lightning wasn't a threat anymore; it was cracking around us, flashes of jagged light coming out of a sky that had already turned midnight black.

As I walked down the final flight of stairs to the main floor, Dahlia Codwell came out of her room, saw me, and fell in beside me. "I'm ticked at you, Tracy," she said.

"What'd I do?"

"You abandoned me last night when I was under the weather."

"You looked okay to me. Actually, you looked a lot better than I did."

"So much for appearances," she said, giving me a warm smile. "I tried to get up after you left, and I couldn't. I staggered out to the stairs and found out I'd forgotten how to climb stairs. The only thing I remembered how to do was to sit down, so I sat down on the stairs. I was paralyzed. I sat there until after one o'clock. If it hadn't been for Jack Scott coming to get me, I'd be sitting there still. He helped me to my room, thank God. Don't ever abandon me that way again. You, sir, are no gentleman."

"That, madam, is a given," I said, and we both laughed and then a crack of lightning blasted close enough that we could smell the ozone it created.

The hall lights flickered, then came back on.

Inside the dining room, she peeled off to get some food from the serving table and I went with her. I was hungry, which was, in itself, an event at least as important as a thunderstorm, because I only really eat every couple of days. This, and good genes, is how I keep my weight down to 220.

We sat together at an empty table, next to Birnbaum's table, and the producer leaned over to me and said, "Well . . . Trace, isn't it? How's it going?"

He was still wearing his Mets jacket. What a dork.

"Fine," I said.

Birnbaum's eyes were glittering, almost as if he had just put drops into them. They were a peculiar shade of grayish brown and I figured, for the first time, that he was older than he looked.

He grinned at me with perfect teeth and said, "Did you find that one of us is a homicidal maniac and tried to brain Roddy with that rock?" He smirked around the table at Sheila and Tami, who were sitting with him. Sheila looked pained.

"No," I said. "But I've taken rock scrapings and sent them off to the FBI for carbon-fourteen tests. If there's anything there, I'll find it out."

Birnbaum nodded sagely. "I've heard of carbon fourteen," he allowed.

He looked toward Sheila Hallowitz as if expecting her to nod sagely too, but Sheila did not look happy. She was staring down at her food, kind of wringing her hands together. Tami looked at me and winked. Well, at least somebody knew that carbon fourteen was a test usually done to determine the age of million-year-old bones, not fingerprints.

The lights flickered again as another bolt of lightning hit nearby. I was hungry and wanted to eat but Birnbaum wanted to talk.

"I guess you're pretty excited with Monday coming." he said.

"I'm always happy to see the next Monday," I said.

"Cast and crew arrives. It'll be real exciting around here, especially for someone who's not in cinema."

"I'll try not to get underfoot."

"Hey, Birnbaum," McCue called from the next table over, where he sat with the Scotts and Ramona Dedley. "Shut up for a while. Can't you see the guy is trying to eat?"

I nodded my thanks to him and turned to my meal. Birnbaum excused himself and left the room, and I decided he must have the weakest kidneys in the world because it seemed he was constantly on his way to the men's room.

When I finished eating, McCue came over to the table. I could feel Dahlia Codwell frosting up as Tony came into our gravitational field.

"Trace, can I talk to you for a minute?" he asked.

I got up and followed him about twenty feet away from the table.

"I'm going out with Doctor Death," he said. "We want to get some new prescriptions."

"Am I going to have to go with you? Are you going to act like a damn fool and get yourself killed?" I asked.

"No, not with Ramona along. And she drives anyway, so you don't have to worry about me."

"Tell her to be careful. This weather doesn't look promising. I don't want anything to happen to you, 'cause I need the fee."

"Don't worry. I'll be on my best behavior too." He whispered. "Ramona's pissed at me. She found out I banged Tami the other night. That's who she was talking to in her room today, warning her to stay away from me."

"Tami? You remember now?"

"Yes, you pain in the ass. I told Dahlia I loved it and she nearly hit me in the head with her martini pitcher. Then I saw Tami making googoo eyes at me and winking and licking her lips and shit like that, and I said, That Trace is a no-good liar. I'll never trust you again."

He turned around as Roddy Quine limped into the dining room and posed dramatically in the entrance doors. He was using a cane he'd gotten from God knows where. Maybe British directors always pack canes with them when they travel, I thought.

McCue left me and ran forward, spread his arms, and shouted to the room, "Let's hear it, ladies and gentlemen, for the Conqueror of Everest."

Quine huffed and puffed and grinned.

McCue left him standing there and went back to his own table to collect Ramona Dedley, and Quine hobbled over and sat in McCue's vacated seat. Jack Scott was smiling at him, but Pamela Scott had the sour kind of look on her face that my ex-wife always got when we were arguing. Which meant it was as constant as the solar wind.

I heard Quine say to Scott, "Humph, humph. Not hurting too badly now, but a close call, what?"

Scott nodded. So did his wife. She was wearing so much makeup I was surprised her face didn't crack from the movement.

"Be difficult for the picture, losing a director now, don't you know?" Quine said. "Close call and all that. Thanked Tony for saving me, you know."

"Directors come and directors go," Scott said. The

grin was frozen on his face and for the first time I realized what an artificial mirthless thing it was. "I'm just glad it wasn't McCue. We lose him . . . Well, no star, no movie. We can always get somebody else to point the camera."

"Yes, yes, humph, humph," Quine said, looking abashed. I thought if he had been looking for sympathy for his terrible leg wound, he certainly wasn't finding any of it at Scott's table.

The lightning cracked again. I could hear the heavy wind whistling against the large windows that surrounded the dining room. Without warning, a sheet of water hit against the glass as the rain started.

Tami Fluff excused herself from the next table. "Powder room," she said.

I got up to make myself a drink and Dahlia said. "Me too. Weak please. One glass. No pitcher. Very dry."

"Yes, Commandant," I mumbled. I saw Arden Harden come into the doorway. He looked around, as if counting heads, then turned and ran toward the stairway.

I was bringing the drinks to the table when he came back into the room and sat at our table.

"I see you put a lock on the hambone's door," he said.

"Yes."

"Why? He doesn't have anything to steal," Harden said.

I ignored him and he said, "I want a lock too. If he gets a lock, I get one. My screenplay revisions are in that room."

"You want a lock, buy a lock," I said. "I'll tell you how to find the hardware store. Five ninety eight plus tax."

Birnbaum leaned over again from the other table. "What's that about a lock, Tracy?"

"I put a lock on McCue's door. Just a precaution."

"Why do you have to take precautions?" he asked.

"I don't know. I'm the cautious type."

"Can't be too cautious," Birnbaum said. "That's what I always say." He looked around for agreement, but Sheila was still just looking down, pushing food around her plate.

Scott came over to our table, smiling, naturally. I always wondered how people are able to smile and talk at the same time, and the ability of singers to smile while warbling absolutely flabbergasted me. I tried it once in front of a bathroom mirror and I had to concentrate so hard on smiling that I forgot the words to the song. And the song was "Happy Birthday." Scott did everything with a smile. Maybe it was what you learned to do when you made your living on television.

"Just wanted to tell all of you that Pamela and I will be going back in the morning. Some personal business." He looked toward the windows and said, "Wow, that's some storm, isn't it?" It wasn't big enough, though, to put a frown on his face.

"We'll be back Sunday night for dinner," he said. "That way I'll be here when the press comes and starts to pester everybody."

"Yeah," I said. "I was wondering how I'd deal with them."

On his personal-rating scale, Scott gave that one Smile Number Three. He said, "Is everything all right, Dahlia?"

"Everything's fine," she said.

"I'll see that Dahlia's fine," Harden said. "Somebody's got to protect the only actor in this film."

That got a Number Two Smile from Scott, who left the table and a few moments later left the dining room with Pamela in tow.

"I'm writing new dialogue for Dahlia," Harden told me. "Good, honest dialogue."

I guess my expression showed that I didn't care if he

wrote her the King James Bible because he turned his back on me and stared at her.

"It's not going to be that naturalistic dialogue, is it?" she asked him.

"What's wrong with that?" Harden said.

"If people wanted to hear natural dialogue, they could sit on a bus and hear it," she said. "People want to hear the great lines. They want actors to make speeches that they wish they could make."

"Speeches never sound natural," Harden said. "That's why Shakespeare stinks."

I always figure it's time to leave when somebody at the table decides that Shakespeare stinks. As I was getting up, Roddy Quine came limping over to sit at the table.

Clyde Snapp stood in the doorway, motioning to me.

"What is it?" I asked.

"I don't know. I got some crazy man on the phone downstairs. Maybe you ought to talk to him."

"What's he want?"

"I don't know. I can't figure it out. He's talking about Tony McCue and murder and I don't know what all."

"Okay," I said. "Let's go see."

The voice over the phone snarled, "Is this McCue?"

"No," I said. "He's out. Who is this?"

"First of all, who is *this*?" the voice growled back. All of a sudden, I was beginning to guess who it was.

"This is Devlin Tracy. At your service."

"Tracy, you moron, what are you doing there?"

"Why, as I live and breathe, it's Detective Razoni, isn't it?"

"Goddamn right, it's Razoni," he said. "I asked you what you're doing there."

"My insurance company has a policy on McCue. I'm keeping an eye on him."

"Good. Then call him to the phone. I want to talk to him," he said.

"Sorry, but he's gone out for the night. Can I help?"

"Remember that accident the other night, the hit-and-run?"

"Yeah."

"Well, the dead guy was wearing McCue's coat and hat. I wanted to ask him about that."

I figured there wasn't any point in lying anymore, so I told him, "I think McCue lost them to him in a saloon bet. Why?"

"Son of a bitch. It took us two freaking days to trace that coat to McCue."

"What for?" I asked. "What difference does it make?"

"It makes this difference. The guy driving the car was a wise guy from up around Albany. We had some guys track it down and it looks like he went to New York City to do a hit. We had the idea that maybe the dead guy wasn't the real target at all. Maybe it was the guy who should have been inside that white hat and coat. Is McCue safe?"

"I don't know. I've told you, he's gone out."

"You're one hell of a bodyguard, Tracy, when you let the guy you're guarding out of your sight. Remind me never to hire you."

"I wouldn't work for you," I said.

"How long are you going to be up there?" Razoni asked.

"I don't know. A couple of weeks," I said.

"Or until McCue dies, which should be pretty quick with you on the job."

"Did you call to insult me?" I said.

"No. Just remember, when you get back to New York, I'm going to want to talk to you and find out how you didn't know the other night that that was McCue's hat and coat. That cost us two days' work, and in my book, that's withholding evidence."

"Yeah? I can just see it now, us all standing in the middle of Fifty-seventh Street and me telling you, Why, I think that coat belongs to Tony McCue the movie star. Razoni, you'd have me in Bellevue."

"I may still have you in Bellevue, Tracy. You tell McCue to call me." He hung up before I could say anything.

Clyde Snapp was looking at me and I said, "Just some nut," and he nodded. But as I walked to the bar, I didn't feel so lighthearted. Where the hell was my head? Here I was thinking that there'd been three attempts to kill Tony McCue and I let him go out drinking, protected only by his psychiatrist. I had no future in this business; that was becoming pretty clear.

I sat at the bar and watched the rain. Birnbaum and Sheila had left the dining room. I had a drink. The lightning storm was still crackling all around us, and when a bolt flashed, it lit up the ground outside the hotel as if a giant flashbulb had gone off.

I was looking out the window when lightning flashed, and I saw two figures walking away from the hotel. More lightning came and I saw it was Jack Scott and Sheila Hallowitz.

Intermittently, as the lightning blazed on, I saw them arguing. Scott was waving his hands, and his head bobbed up and down. She seemed to shrink visibly while he was talking, and I realized that he wasn't talking, he was yelling. Then, wonder of wonders, I saw her yelling back.

Scott obviously was not used to being yelled at. He should live with Chico, I thought. Scott listened for a few seconds, then stomped angrily away, walking rapidly back up the path toward the hotel.

In the lightning flash, I saw Sheila standing on the path, looking after him.

And then a crack of lightning hit and all the lights went out.

23

If I were a betting man, I'd have to say that it wasn't the first time the lights had ever gone off in the Canestoga Hotel because the shouts of confusion had barely stopped when Clyde Snapp was in the dining room with a box filled with kerosene lamps.

"Just a power line down, folks," he said. "It should be fixed soon. Meanwhile, we've got some emergency lights here."

I lit one and put it on the bar, and he lit another and put it on the table where Dahlia was sitting with Harden and Quine.

"There's candles in all the rooms for emergencies," he said to me. "I'm just going to put these lamps on the landings and I'll tell everybody where the candles are."

"You need any help?" I asked.

"Np."

Drinking in the dark isn't a bad experience. Smoking in the dark is worthless because, without seeing it, you can't really taste the smoke. But vodka, I found, is vodka no matter what the lighting situation is. It's one of those things that are good to know.

Outside, the lightning finally seemed to be subsiding and the rain was lessening in intensity.

Sheila Hallowitz came into the dining room, saw the people sitting at the table, and came to sit at the bar with me.

She looked nervous as she said, "You mind if I join you?"

"Of course not."

She giggled nervously. "All my life I've been afraid to be alone in the dark. And that candle doesn't really help in the room. I thought I'd hang out here with people until Biff comes back or until the lights come on."

"No explanation necessary," I said. "Would you like a drink?"

"Sure." She thought for a moment. "How about Seven and Seven."

As I made the drink, I said, "Not much of a drinker, are you?"

"How can you tell?"

"By the drink. No one who really drinks drinks Seven and Seven. It's a kid's drink, the first thing they learn to order because they think it makes them sound grown-up. And it's sweet, to boot."

I handed her the drink just as a gale of loud professional laughter came from Dahlia Codwell at the rear table.

"Seem to be enjoying themselves, don't they?" I said.

"I guess so," she said.

"But why do I get the idea that those two men are being conned by that woman?"

Sheila stared at me for a moment and then suddenly grinned, an honest smile that made her look pretty in the flickering light from the kerosene lamp. "Because you're absolutely right. They are," she said. She sipped from her glass cautiously, as if it might contain battery acid.

I had made the drink weak and it apparently passed muster because she smiled again. I waited for her to say something. Most people are made nervous by silence, and if you wait long enough, they'll tell you things they didn't really want to tell you, just to fill up the dead air.

"Dahlia's trying to get her part puffed up," she said.

"Sounds like she's succeeding," I said as another burst of laughter flitted across the room.

"She's just spinning her wheels," Sheila said. "Biff will be the judge of who says what and where the camera is."

"I thought producers just signed checks," I said.

"Not Biff. Not the new wave of producers," she said. "These are people who've written scripts and learned to direct, so when they produce a movie, make no mistake, they're in charge of everything about it. Dahlia's wasting her time." She had a vague accent-free voice that I thought stamped her as a native Californian. "Anyway, Arden won't do anything to expand her part. He's crazy about Tami."

"I didn't know she was Polish," I said.

"Polish? What do you mean?"

"I thought only Polish starlets went out with the screenwriter," I said.

"Oh, I get it. Little joke," she said, but she didn't laugh. I didn't think there was much of a sense of humor there. "Arden actually discovered her, working in his lawyer's office. He was doing a small movie for an independent producer and he insisted she get a bit part. Well, she got some work after that, one of the jobs in another movie he wrote, and he's been chasing her all this time. He thinks she has some kind of obligation to him, and she doesn't see it that way. But that's why he acts crazy when he thinks she's with McCue or anybody else."

"The kind who'd kill for jealousy," I said, and she nodded.

"Is he a good writer?" I asked.

"Mr. Tracy, my degree is from the University of Chicago in classical literature. I find it hard to call anybody who writes films a good writer."

"Then no one likes him or his script. Why do you keep him around? He sure isn't exactly a bundle of fun."

"Would you mind if I had another drink?" she said.

"No. Sure." I got up to make it for her. "You were saying?"

"Arden is bankable. People will put up money if they see his name involved with a film."

"Even if his script is lousy?"

"Being bankable has nothing to do with talent. Some people get a reputation for being bankable even if they're involved in nothing but flops. You get a better reputation being involved with a sixty-million-dollar movie that lost fifty-nine million dollars than you do if you were involved with a two-million-dollar movie that made ten million dollars. Try to figure it."

"Too tough for me. I'm an Easterner. So his name has raised the money you need for the movie?"

"Well, his and Jack Scott's have helped," she said.

I made the drink twice as strong, and when I set it down in front of her, I said, "Last couple of nights, I've noticed Scott. Is there anything wrong with him?"

I watched her closely: her lips tightened and she seemed to be biting down on the inside of them.

"What do you mean?" she said.

"I don't know. We talked a little, but he didn't seem pleased. He always seems like something is wrong with this film."

Sheila didn't answer right away. Then she shook her

head and sipped her drink. "He's never mentioned anything wrong to me. Nothing's wrong. Nothing."

She looked away but I saw a tear glistening in the corner of her eye, an orange dot illuminated by the kerosene lamp.

"Where you come from, do people always cry when nothing's wrong?" I asked.

She wiped her eyes with the back of her left hand. "Sorry. Just some personal problems," she said. "Nothing to do with the movie. I've got to go now. I'm not feeling so good." She stood up and swayed slightly, "I don't know if I can really walk. I don't ever drink."

"I'll help you up to your room," I said. I led her up the two flights of steps to the suite she shared with Birnbaum. He was not in the room and the door was unlocked. A two-inch-thick candle burned on the dresser. I helped Sheila to the sofa and asked, "Will you be all right here?"

"Sure. I feel better now."

"Okay. Have a good night."

Just as I was backing out the door, the lights came back on.

"Thank God," Sheila said.

"I can also pull rabbits out of hats," I said.

"Fixing the lights is good enough. Thanks very much."

As I walked back down the hall, the door to the last of the rooms opened and Tami Fluff looked out. She was wearing a long blue satin robe.

I nodded, not knowing what to expect.

But she smiled at me. "Hello, Tracy. Produce any good movies lately?"

"I'm sorry about that," I said. "You know it wasn't my doing."

"I know. What are you doing now?"

"Walking down the hall, basically," I said.

"Come on in."

"Is it safe?"

"What do you mean?"

"I don't want Harden swinging his typewriter and kneecapping me."

"He's a great argument for pest control, isn't he? Come on in." She closed the door behind me and locked it. "There's no significance to the door being locked," she said. "I just don't want Arden crashing in here without an invitation."

"He does that, huh?"

"He thinks he owns me. You know he had nothing to do with me getting the part in this picture."

I shrugged. I didn't really know anything, and in truth I didn't really care.

"He didn't," she said. "I auditioned and got it before he even knew about it. Birnbaum signed me. You want a drink?"

"Do I look like a drinking man?"

"All I've got is Scotch."

"Do I look like a nitpicker? Scotch away."

She had a refrigerator, I noticed. My room must have been part of the Canestoga Hotel ghetto. She had a refrigerator and McCue's suite had a refrigerator. Maybe everybody did except me. No, I decided. I hadn't seen a refrigerator in the suite Sheila shared with Birnbaum. That eased the pain a little.

She popped ice into two hotel glasses and poured Scotch over them. "Here," she said, walking toward me. Her sleek legs peeked out from the front opening of the robe and I hoped this would not be a seduction scene. I was going straight. Why didn't people believe that? Did I look like the kind of person who never went straight?

I took my glass and she said, "Well, here's to Hollywood."

"Here's to you," I said. "I hope dis pitcha makes you da biggest star in da whole foimament of Hollywood."

"God, you sound like every casting-couch producer who ever lived. Any reason you wish me good luck?"

"Because I suspect that you're the only person here whose success I wouldn't resent," I said.

She was still standing in front of me, uncomfortably close. "That include Tony?"

"I can't wish him stardom. He's already got it, and good for him. He's a big kid but not malicious. But the others? That's a different story."

"You mean you don't like Arden Harden, the Bard of Beverly?"

"A little nasty for my taste," I said. "And the Brit with the wooden teeth acts like Nigel Bruce doing Watson. I wish the rock *had* fallen on his head. And I think Birnbaum's a dork, and Scott and his wife look at me like I'm a leaky garbage bag that has to be taken out."

"You must like Dahlia, though. She's made a career out of getting men to like her."

"She's a user," I said. "She's downstairs now trying to get Harden and Quine to puff up her part." I looked hard at her face for a reaction, but there wasn't any.

She sipped her drink, then said, "She can have Harden and Quine. I'd rather have Tony on my side."

"Is he?" I asked.

She shrugged. "I talked to him last night. He likes me better than he likes Codwell. I think he'll resist any changes that give her a bigger role than me."

"Good. Then I guess it was worth it."

"What was worth it?"

"Sleeping with him," I said.

She looked at me as if to see if I was bluffing. Then she nodded and said, "It sure was."

"Thanks for the drink," I said as I got to my feet.

She leaned forward against me. "Do you have to leave now?" she said.

"No, but I'd better," I said.

"Why?"

"Because if I wait any longer, I don't think I'll be able to leave," I said. "You're very beautiful."

"You have a woman?" she asked.

"She has me," I said.

"She must be special."

"She is. Very special. And I can't stop drinking for her and I can't stop smoking and I won't exercise and I can't stay out of trouble for her, but at least I don't have to go around screwing around behind her back."

"How very old-fashioned," she said.

"I'm stuck with it," I said. "At least this week."

"If you change your mind, let me know."

I nodded and walked out, feeling very righteous. And very stupid.

In the hallway, I met Clyde, who was picking up the kerosene lamps he had placed on the landings. He looked at me and winked. Somehow that made me feel even worse.

24

I was starting to worry a little. It was past eleven o'clock and no sign of McCue. I stood at the front door of the hotel, but his Rolls-Royce wasn't in the parking lot. Then I saw Pamela Scott's head appear from between parked cars and she walked toward the front door.

I held the door open for her. "Hello, Mrs. Scott."

"Hello," she mumbled. She was still wearing all that heavy makeup she'd worn for dinner.

"Nice night finally, isn't it?" I said, but she didn't answer as she walked away toward the stairs.

Well, hell, it *was* a nice night. The storm had stopped and the weather seemed warmer. I strolled out to the front gate and tried to talk to the guard for a while, but he hadn't seen McCue since dinnertime, and I wasn't a star and so he was more interested in reading his *Playboy* magazine than talking to me.

When I got back to the hotel, I saw Clyde Snapp crouched at the rear of a Cadillac in the parking lot.

"What's up, Clyde?"

"Just changing a tire. Mrs. Scott noticed she had a flat."

"Don't let me stop you." I hate changing tires and I hate even thinking about changing tires. Idly I decided to stroll the grounds a little.

The moonlight was hard, brittle, as I picked my way along the path behind the hotel, strolling down toward the lake.

In the clearing where Quine had been injured, the big round rock still lay. It had been up on top of the ledge for what . . . Snapp said sixty years. Now it was down here and it'd probably stay *here* for sixty years, unless somebody had a good reason for moving it.

I scrambled up to the top of the shelf the round rock had fallen from, and squatted there, feeling the rock's wet surface with my hand, thinking myself pretty much an idiot, because what could I hope to find?

The moonlight made the world look dead, I was thinking, and then I heard someone walking along the path, below and to the right of me. The moon passed behind a cloud and the night suddenly grew very dark and for a moment I don't think I would have minded carrying Sarge's big elephant gun.

Whoever it was was in the small clearing below me. The cloud swept clean the face of the moon and it seemed to shine brighter than it had before.

I looked over the edge of the rock and saw the face of Pamela Scott looking up at me.

"Hello, Mr. Tracy," she said. She smiled; her teeth glinted like Dracula's in the high moon's light.

"Mrs. Scott."

"Pamela, please," she said. "It's a beautiful night, isn't it?"

"Yes, it is."

There was silence for a while and she said, "Are you coming down or am I climbing up there?"

I came down the side of the rock to the small clearing, and she said, "I thought I might as well enjoy the peace and quiet now. Once they start shooting next week, this place will be filled with platforms and lights and power lines and stuff. It'll look like a freight yard."

"It might be fun to watch," I said.

"I guess so," she said. "I was going to walk down to the dock. Walk along with me?"

"Sure," I said.

We stepped side by side along the broad path and she pulled her light raincoat tighter around her.

"You know you're the only precinct I haven't heard from," I said.

"What do you mean?"

"I've heard what everybody else thinks about this film, except for you."

"What *does* everyone else think about it?"

"They all seem to think that it's an awful screenplay," I said.

"Well, Jack and I don't. Oh, sure, it needs some work. But we think it can be a blockbuster. We've got all our personal resources in this film. That tells you how serious we are about it."

"By resources, you mean money?" I asked.

"Sure."

"I thought producers never put up money. That you let other people take the risk."

"And sometimes, if not enough of them are willing to take the risk, you have to commit yourself to it," she said. "That's what we've done. If Jack seems a little abrupt sometimes, now you know why."

We had reached the dock and stood at its base looking out over the lake. Only the ripples reflected the moonbeams, like light peeking through rips in a piece of black fabric.

Pamela Scott shuddered from the cold.

"I'm surprised it was hard to raise money for this film," Trace asked. "I thought with Tony McCue's name, all you had to do was spread the word."

"Sometimes it works that way, sometimes it doesn't. This one didn't, so we had to pick up the slack," she said. "If it works, we're golden. If not . . . Well, there's always the typing pool to go back to." She shivered again. "I'm cold," she said.

"I am too," I said. "The next time we make this trip, we'd better remember to bring a Saint Bernard with brandy."

We walked back slowly and I left her at the front door to their suite.

A flight up, I heard voices and I paused on the landing to listen. They were coming from Tami's room, and since I couldn't hear well enough, I walked over closer to the door.

I recognized the voices as Tami's and Arden Harden's.

"I think you've got an obligation to me," he said. There was an angry edge to his voice.

"I think you're dreaming. Arden, you helped me get started. For that, thanks. But that's all. No more. Don't think there should be any more because there won't be any more."

"So you're just going to sleep with anybody you think can help you," he said.

"Something like that," she agreed.

"You're a bitch, Tami. Just a bitch. I'd like to wring your neck."

I waited for a moment in case he tried to wring her neck, but instead I heard her say, "You ought to get out of here. Now."

And he said, "I'm going. But I won't forget."

And I took off and ran up the steps to the next floor. The lock was still on Tony McCue's door and I was beginning to think I should have gone with them, after all. For all I knew, Ramona Dedley was a whacko drunk driver and they were lying, pieces of unrecognizable chopmeat, in a ditch somewhere.

I walked back to my room just as Harden turned the corner.

"Oh, you," he said.

"Just turning in," I said.

"Did Pamela Scott find you? She was up here looking for you."

"Yeah. I found her. Thanks."

"Think nothing of it," he said, went into his room, and slammed the door.

I lay down on the bed just to rest for a while and fell immediately asleep. Later, I heard a sound and glanced at my watch. One-forty A.M.

I shook my head to wake up. The sound was Tony McCue and he was singing:

"You can tell a brute who boozes,

By the company he chooses.

And the pig got up and slowly walked away."

"Shhhhh." That was Ramona Dedley's voice.

They were in the hall. I heard thumping on the door of his suite and knew what had happened. The idiot, naturally, had lost the key to the lock. I got up from the bed and fished the spare padlock key from my jacket pocket and went out into the hall.

McCue was seated on the floor in front of his door, legs outstretched on the worn old carpet. "It's no use, Ramona," he said. "We're hopelessly lost. Are you sure this is my room?"

Ramona saw me coming toward them and shrugged.

"Trace, old buddy," McCue said. "Let's have a drink."

"You mean you left some in the world?" I said.

"Do I detect pique? Is that pique?" McCue said.

"That's the grumble of a man who wants to get some

sleep." I reached over him and unlocked the padlock and stuck it and the key in my pants pocket.

"I'll see you in the morning," I said.

McCue wrapped both his arms around my left leg.

"Don't leave me now," he whimpered. "She wants to do terrible things to me. Help me. Save me."

"Remington Steele episode. July 26, 1986. Pierce Brosnan and Stephanie Zimbalist," I said.

"Aaaah, you're a pain in the ass." He waved an arm at me in disgust. "You know when you're grown-up?"

"When?"

"When your friends don't want to come out and play anymore."

I looked at Ramona. "Can you handle him?" I said.

"I'm used to it," she answered. "No problem."

"Get some sleep, Tony," I said.

I went back into my room, undressed, and turned off the light. Through the wall, I could hear McCue roaring.

"Not a goddamn ice cube. Just piss-warm water in the bowl. What kind of hotel is this?"

"If you want ice cubes," she said, "you have to put water in the tray."

"Bullshit," he shouted. "That's woman's work."

"Tony, come to bed," her voice answered softly.

"Without goddamn ice for a goddamn drink, what goddamn choice do I have?" he yelled.

Then all was quiet for a while and I thought they had gone to sleep.

Then I heard Ramona cry out, "Oh Tony. Yes, yes."

With all that booze in him too. Who ever said a movie star's life was easy?

25

"What? What?"

Somebody was in my room shaking me.

"What? What?"

"Get up, Tracy."

"Who is it?" It was just starting to get light and I couldn't focus my eyes yet real well.

"Snapp. Get up. Something's happened."

"What? What?"

"Get your pants on and come downstairs to the kitchen," he said. He left the room even before I had my feet on the floor.

Down in the kitchen, I found Snapp standing in front of the stainless-steel table along the right side of the wall. The door to one of the dumbwaiters was open.

He pointed to the opening. "In here," he said.

I came over closer and saw a pair of feet dangling only about eighteen inches above the floor of the dumbwaiter shaft.

I turned to Snapp. "It's Scott," he said. "The TV guy."

"Dead?" I said. I still wasn't functioning real well.

What the hell did I think? He was alive and working on a new form of exercise?

"Deader than Kelso's nuts," Snapp said.

I pulled the stainless-steel table away from the way, leaned in, and looked up the shaft.

"He's dead," Snapp said. "You can feel him. He's colder than a freshwater clam."

"You got a flashlight?" I said.

He slapped one into my hand like a relay-team baton. I climbed up into the opening of the shaft. The knees of my trousers got wet from something. For a moment I thought it was blood, but my hands felt water. There was a plastic bowl, the kind margarine is packaged in, in the corner of the dumbwaiter shaft. I got to my feet and shined the light upward.

Jack Scott's face was only about a foot from mine. His eyes were open and so was his mouth. His body stank in the long narrow shaft that rose four stories above this basement.

I leaned against the wall for a better look and saw that the dumbwaiter rope had been twisted once around his throat and his head was bent off to the side as if his neck had been broken.

"We ought to take him down, I guess," Snapp said. "I didn't want to do it, though, until you got here."

"Why me?"

"You're a private detective. I didn't want to go destroying no clues or nothing. Should we take him down now?"

"Leave him. Let's call the police," I said.

"I just did. He'll be here any minute."

I climbed out of the dumbwaiter. "What the hell's this water?" I said.

Snapp shrugged. "Old building. Sometimes you get a leaky pipe. Or maybe rain from that storm."

I said, "I wonder what happened to him. What the hell's he doing in the dumbwaiter?"

"Happens once in a while," he said.

"This is pretty common for you?" I said. "People get hanged in your dumbwaiter all the time?"

"Np," he said. He had taken a large wad of paper towels and was wiping up the water from the bottom of the shaft. He stuffed the towels into the plastic container and dumped the bundle into a plastic garbage bag. "No, what I mean is sometimes people get drunk and decide they's Tarzan and start trying to climb the ropes. That's why I closed off all those doors in the rooms upstairs." He shook his head. "Never had one get hanged before," he said.

"How'd you find him anyway?"

"I was up, starting to get breakfast ready." He pointed to a large steel bowl filled with a couple of dozen eggs. "And I saw a little dribble of water coming out from under the door. So I opened the door—I didn't bother to lock them down here because *I* ain't gonna play Tarzan—and I saw his freaking feet right in front of me, swinging back and forth. Then I climbed in, like you did." He brushed his knees. "Got wet just like you did too. I felt him. Cold and stiff."

"I'd better tell the others," I said.

"Guess so."

Birnbaum was wearing a sweatsuit and his face was soaked with perspiration when he answered my soft knock on the door. The sofa behind him had been opened into a bed. It was rumpled, unmade, and his barbells were in the middle of the floor.

He called, "Come in. What gets you up at this hour?" he said as he hoisted a heavy barbell over his head.

"You'd better put that damn thing down before I tell you."

He set the weight softly on the bed pillows he had placed on the floor to muffle the sound of the heavy weights dropping onto the carpet.

"Jack Scott's dead," I said.

He stared at me, blankly, no expression on his face. "Say what?" he finally said.

"There's been an accident. Jack Scott's dead. Come on."

Birnbaum looked inside the dusty dumbwaiter shaft too.

"It's Jack, all right."

"We know that," I said. "What we don't know is what the hell he's doing there."

"What the Christ do I know?" Birnbaum snapped. "I'm sorry, Tracy. I'm just shocked. I don't know . . . it's just too much . . . I don't know. Have you told Pamela?"

I shook my head. "I was waiting for a volunteer," I said.

"I guess it's my job," he said.

I followed him up to the suite the Scotts had shared on the level above the main floor. Pamela Scott had been sleeping: her hair was tousled and her face not made up. She wore a heavy chenille bathrobe when she opened the door.

"Hello, Biff." She nodded to me. "Jack's already gone, I guess."

When there was no response, she hesitated, then said, "What is it? What is it?"

Birnbaum took her arm and led her toward the sofa. I followed as he sat her down and said, "There's been an accident."

"Accident? What?" She looked at Birnbaum, then at me, then back at Birnbaum. "Jack?" she said, her voice rising in pitch.

Birnbaum nodded. "There's been an accident, Pamela. Jack's dead."

She screamed, a long keening shriek, then slipped back out of Birnbaum's arms and fell onto the sofa. I noticed her skin looked blotchy.

"She's fainted," Birnbaum told me, quite unnecessarily.

I walked to the refrigerator, but the ice tray was empty. I found a can of frozen orange juice and wrapped it in a napkin from atop the dresser and touched the cold compress to Pamela Scott's temples, one side after the other.

"Maybe I should get the doctor," Birnbaum said.

"No. You stay here. You're a friend. I'll get Ramona," I said.

I ran up the two flights of stairs to McCue's room, just as I began to realize I'd better check McCue and make sure he had not had an accident too.

The suite's door was locked from the inside and I pounded on it. Arden Harden stuck his head out the door on the far end of the hall, nearest the stairs, and shouted, "What the hell is that racket? Quiet it down there, Tracy. I'm trying to sleep."

"Get back inside that room before I step on you," I snapped, and kept pounding.

A few seconds later, Ramona, who had obviously dressed quickly in the clothes she had been wearing the night before, answered.

"Oh . . . Trace," she said.

"Is Tony all right?"

"Yes, of course. He's still sleeping."

"All right. Can you come downstairs? We need you."

"What's happened?"

"Jack Scott's died. And his wife just fainted."

"Oh, dear. Let's go."

She followed me down the hallway. As we passed the door to Harden's room, it opened a crack and I could see the little writer watching us as we went by.

26

Pamela Scott had been revived. She sat on the bed with Birnbaum, who had his arm around her shoulder. Tears streamed down her cheeks.

Ramona Dedley shooed him off the bed and helped the woman lie down, covered her with a light blanket, and took her pulse. She nodded and said, "You've just got to rest for a while. I'll bring a sedative down from my room."

"I'll be all right, Doctor," Pamela said.

"I'm awfully sorry," Ramona said. "I'm just so sorry."

"I know. Thank you for your kindness," Mrs. Scott said as she turned her face away, toward the window, and lay unmoving.

I walked back out into the living room and picked up the can of orange juice. Its cardboard sides were softer now and I put it back into the freezer.

Birnbaum came over and we stood at the window, looking out over the front entrance to the hotel. "I guess we should tell the others," he said.

"What did Mrs. Scott say?" I asked.

"She said she went to bed and her husband wasn't

back. She didn't hear him come in, but sometimes he sleeps on the couch when he comes in late so he doesn't wake her up."

"But the couch wasn't opened, so Scott was someplace else last night," I said.

"I guess so. Or maybe he just didn't sleep. Maybe he was here writing letters or something." I followed him over to the dumbwaiter door and noticed that the screw used to lock the door had been removed. Birnbaum pulled the door open and we leaned over, looking inside. All I saw were the ropes in front of me, then peering down, Scott's body only eight feet below me, hanging from the rope. I wondered why the hell Scott had opened the door in the first place. It didn't make any sense.

"We've got to go down and take that body down," I said softly to Birnbaum, "before she looks into this shaft."

"Yeah," he said.

Behind us, there was a whoop outside, and through the window we saw a black-and-white car with a panel of red-and-blue roof lights roaring into the grounds at high speed.

"Good," Birnbaum said. "The cops can take the body down."

The cop wasn't just a cop. He was the duly elected sheriff of Cawonga County. His name was Len Tillis, he was big and fat and very deferential to Clyde Snapp, and while he may have been a genius at winning the hearts of the voters in an election, he didn't have a brain in his head about evidence because he clambered into the kitchen dumbwaiter without even so much as taking a picture, struggled to unwrap the heavy rope from around Scott's neck, and then passed the body out to Snapp, who laid it on the stainless-steel food-preparation table, where it looked like a Thanksgiving turkey awaiting cooking.

"That's Jack Scott, all right. I seen him on television," Tillis said, wiping the dust from his hands onto his uniform. "He looks different."

"He's dead now," I said.

"Sure is," Sheriff Tillis said. "So you found the body, Mr. Snapp?"

"That's right."

"How do you think it got there?"

"Don't know."

"You have any ideas?" The sheriff looked at Birnbaum and me, and we both shook our heads.

"Well, it sure as hell ain't no murder," the sheriff said, "and it's a damn funny way to commit suicide. I guess some kind of accident."

"It's a damn funny accident too," I said, but Sheriff Tillis didn't respond and I got the feeling that this was as far as he had ever gone in an investigation of a sudden death. I felt sorry for him.

"Sheriff," I said.

"Aaaayp. What's your name?"

"Devlin Tracy."

"He's a private detective from New York City," Snapp said.

"A gumshoe, huh?" Sheriff Tillis said. "Don't imagine this is much of a job for you." He hooked his thumbs into his belt, although his stomach was so big that I hadn't thought anything else, even thumbs, could fit there.

"Don't imagine," I said.

"He came here to protect some people," Snapp said.

"You didn't do much of a job, Tracy," the sheriff said.

I nodded at the corpse. "He wasn't the one I was supposed to protect. Can I make a suggestion, Sheriff?"

"Just as long as it don't involve breaking no law. I know how you private dicks are, you know."

"It doesn't. I just wanted to tell you that Mr. Birnbaum and I talked to Scott's wife upstairs and she didn't know if he had come back to the room last night or not. We have a hotel full of people and they're going to have to be told about the death. Why don't you make arrangements to move the body and then question them? See who saw Scott last. See if he was roaring drunk or something. That might answer your question on how he died."

"I don't need you to tell me how to run my investigation, Shamus," the sheriff said. He had been watching too much television.

"You could listen to him, Len," said Snapp. "He's a pretty bright fella."

"I'll do it my way. I wanna question the people who are staying here," Sheriff Tillis said. "But first I'll have somebody remove this body to the hospital."

"Good plan, Sheriff," I said. "Much better than mine." Snapp winked at me and I glanced at my watch. It seemed as if I'd been up half a day already, but it was only just past seven-thirty A.M.

I told Birnbaum, "You ought to let everybody know what's going on."

"Let's get them down to the dining room. We can tell them all at once," Birnbaum said. He shook his head. "Then I've got to figure out what to do with this film."

"Don't we believe anymore in 'the show must go on'?" I asked.

"I believe in it. I don't know if the investors do."

Ramona Dedley came into the kitchen. She stopped short, just for a moment, when she saw Scott's body, then walked over to it.

"I'm really sorry, Mrs. Scott," Sheriff Tillis said. He took his hat off and held it in his hands.

Ramona felt around Scott's throat and lifted his head slightly.

"Broken neck," she said.

"You don't have to do this, Mrs. Scott," the sheriff said. He touched her on the shoulder. "We'll do all this at the hospital."

"I'd say he's been dead at least eight hours. There's some rigor in the body and a lot of pooling in the lower extremities."

"Really, little lady. You ought to go up and lie down. We'll see to your husband's remains."

Ramona turned as if she saw him for the first time. "Who are you?" she asked.

"Sheriff Len Tillis at your service, Mrs. Scott. If there's anything we can do . . ."

"Yes. Stop calling me Mrs. Scott. She's asleep upstairs under sedation. I'm Doctor Ramona Dedley."

"You're a doctor?"

"Yes."

"You're a woman."

"With that kind of perception, you'll have no trouble at all figuring out what happened here," she said. "I'm going to get dressed," she told me. "If you need me, just call."

"We're going to have everybody meet in the dining room right away so we can break the news," I said.

"If you see anybody, tell them to meet us in the dining room," Birnbaum said.

She nodded and left the room.

"A doctor. I'll be damned," Sheriff Tillis said.

"Len, you are a giant old fool," Clyde Snapp said. He was cleaning his nails with a pocketknife. "Didn't you ever hear of a lady doctor?"

"Aaay-p. Sure I heard of them, Mr. Snapp. I just never met any of them, and pretty ones at that. I'm going to call for the ambulance." He pronounced it am-byoo-LANCE.

"Yeah. Do that," Birnbaum said, and started upstairs.

I followed him a minute or so later and met Arden Harden coming down the steps to the main floor.

"What the hell's going on here? I heard sirens," he said.

"Jack Scott's dead," I said.

Harden said, "Really?"

I nodded and he turned and started back up the stairs at a trot.

"Where are you going?"

"I've got to call my agent."

"Why?" I asked.

"I don't know. I always call my agent when something happens," he said. "Have to see what my rights are, I guess."

"Get back to the dining room right away. There's a meeting," I said.

"Soon as I call my agent," he called back.

I walked upstairs slowly, opened McCue's unlocked door, and went into the bedroom, where he was sprawled out, naked, on top of the sheets.

I shook him. "Hey, bare-ass, wake up."

He fought to open one eye, then fought an even greater battle to focus it. "Trace. Is it cocktail hour already?"

"There's an emergency. Get some clothes on and get down to the dining room right away."

"What? What emergency?"

"Just hurry downstairs," I said. I didn't feel much like talking to him now and I thought it'd be easier to get him downstairs if I didn't tell him what was going on.

That took care of the third floor. McCue was getting

up and Harden knew about it. I was the only other person staying on that floor.

I walked down a level and saw Birnbaum coming out of Tami Fluff's room. "I got them all on the way," Birnbaum said. "Will you get Quine and Dahlia downstairs?" he asked. "I want to change."

I could understand that. He probably had a special Mets jacket suitable for funerals.

On the first floor of bedrooms, next to the Scotts' suite, Quine finally answered my pounding on the door. The silly nit was wearing a long nightshirt and a flannel cap. There was something different about his face, and it took me a moment to realize he wasn't wearing his false teeth. Why would someone wear false teeth that made him look like a horse? If you were going to wear a plate, why not wear one that made you look human?

"Err, err, err, err . . ." Quine started. That didn't bother me; I had trouble speaking English in the morning too. "What is it, old man? Humph, grumph, err, err, err, err."

He sounded like a volcano giving its first-warning rumbles before erupting. Something smelled bad and I realized it was his cologne.

"Jack Scott," I said. "He's had an accident. Birnbaum has called a meeting right away in the dining room."

"Accident, eh? Had one myself yesterday. Hope his wasn't as bad as that. Cut my leg up real bad."

"His was worse. He's dead," I said.

"Dead, eh? Humph, grumph, err, err, err. Be there as soon as I don my trousers. And call my agent."

"Just hurry up," I said.

I pounded on Dahlia Codwell's door but got no answer. The door was locked, so I pounded some more. Maybe she was in the shower, I thought, and couldn't hear me. I went into the dining room and poured myself a drink. Actually, I had gone in for coffee, but I figured it was going to be a long day of dealing with these looneytoons and a drink might start it off better.

As I stood at the bar, the hotel's guests started drifting in.

Harden said to me, as if he thought I would care, "It's okay. Everything's all right."

"You brought him back to life?"

"No, but my contract is with the production company, not with him personally. If we make the movie, I stay."

"I'll rest a lot easier now," I said. "I was really worried about that."

When Quine came in, I couldn't tell if he had called his agent or the wardrobe department because he was wearing jodhpurs and a white shirt with an ascot.

Tami must have heard about the death because she had on a black dress, presumably suitable for mourning, because its hemline dropped all the way to midthigh.

Birnbaum was still dressed in his sweatsuit but his eyes were sparkling now and he seemed full of energy. Whatever he drank, I'd like to get some of it.

Ramona and Sheila came in together.

They scattered themselves at tables with coffee and watched Birnbaum, who paced back and forth at the side of the room. Behind him, the windows overlooked the grounds leading to the lake.

"Where's Dahlia?" he asked me.

"I'll try again." I walked up the flight of steps and pounded on her door again. It opened with a fast pull.

Dahlia was wearing a bathrobe but was fully made up. Maybe she slept in her makeup. Maybe everyone did.

"Were you doing all that damned pounding on my door a few minutes ago?" she growled in her husky voice.

"Yes."

"What the hell for? I need some sleep, or hadn't you morons noticed?"

I watched her face carefully as I said, "Jack Scott is dead."

"Dead?" She looked truly surprised and shocked. Then she threw an arm up, the back of her wrist to her forehead, and I wondered why people did that. What kind of gesture was that anyway? It didn't exist anywhere except on a stage. But I thought she was really surprised, except that's the trouble in dealing with actors: you never know when they're lying.

"Yes. An accident. Please come down to the dining room. Birnbaum's called a meeting."

"As soon as I call my agent," she said.

"Why not let your agent wait ten minutes while you find out what happened, so you really have something to tell him?" I suggested.

"I'll think about it while I'm putting my clothes on."

"Hurry up. They're waiting for you."

"Don't think I want you pounding on my door all the time," she said. "This was an exceptional occasion."

"Don't hold your breath, lady," I said. I didn't really mind. She was a boozer, and it isn't really uncommon for boozers to be nasty when they first wake up.

I told Birnbaum that she would be down in a minute.

"Where's McCue?" he asked.

"Should be on his way down."

McCue came pouring through the dining-room doors. "Fifteen men on a dead man's chest . . .

"Yo ho ho and a bottle of rum . . . Good morning, my children. Why the long faces?"

"There's been a tragedy," Birnbaum said, dropping the corners of his mouth, trying to look sad.

"Can't be an important tragedy," McCue said. "I feel fine."

"Shut up, you self-centered hambone," Harden yelled out. "Jack Scott's dead."

"How could you tell?" McCue asked.

"Please," Birnbaum implored. "Will you sit down, Tony? We have to talk about this."

McCue walked over to me near the bar. I scooped some ice cubes into a glass and handed it to him along with the bottle of gin.

Dahlia Codwell walked in through the door, paused for a moment, then called out, "Oh, God. It's so awful." Then she fainted. I wondered if her agent had told her to do that.

McCue said, "Quick somebody. Make her a martini."

But nobody went over to help her and she revived herself.

27

"I know we're all shocked by the tragedy," Biff Birnbaum said. "Nobody knows how it happened."

"How what happened, old chap?" Roddy Quine said.

"Jack was found dead this morning, hanging from the rope in the dumbwaiter shaft," Birnbaum said.

"How'd it happen?" Quine asked.

"He just said nobody knows how it happened," Harden snapped. "Damn fool."

"It was some kind of tragic accident," Birnbaum said. "Apparently Jack suffered a broken neck and died. Mrs. Scott is now under sedation from Doctor Dedley."

I noticed Clyde Snapp and Sheriff Tillis enter the room and stand quietly in the back.

"The sheriff is here," Birnbaum said, "and perhaps he'll be able to throw a little light on the death for us after he completes his investigation. I know you'll all cooperate."

"What about the filming?" Dahlia Codwell asked, apparently recovered from her attack of grief.

"This is no time to talk business," Birnbaum said, then began to talk business. "I don't know what the investors will decide, and so the fate of the film is up to them. As you know, this film is being developed with private money, and if that money leaves, then the film will have to be scrapped."

"If it goes ahead, I'm in the contract. My agent told me," Harden said.

"As I said, that'll be up to the investors. The rest of the cast and crew are supposed to be here on Monday, and I'm just going to let them come ahead. It's my plan to keep shooting until the money we have on hand runs out. That may force anybody who's wavering to stay in, rather than back out and lose everything he's put up till then."

"Only a fool throws good money after bad," McCue whispered to me at the bar.

"Another thing," Birnbaum said. "As soon as word of this gets out, I'm sure we're going to be bombarded by press people." He looked toward the entrance. "Mr. Snapp, will you be sure to keep the guards on the gate and make sure they allow no one in except those of us who are connected with the film? And, of course, the police."

Snapp nodded.

"I think it would be best," Birnbaum said, "if I made all the statements to the press. This is a tragedy. Let's don't make it a travesty by everybody sounding off to the media, if you don't mind. We owe it to poor Pamela not to make her husband's death into a circus. And I know you'll all cooperate with Sheriff Tillis, who's in the back of the room."

Tillis had been quietly looking over the room. Now he hitched up his belt and walked toward Birnbaum.

The producer said, "One final thing. Jack Scott was my friend and my partner for ten years. I thought of him as a brother, the brother I never had when I was growing up on the streets of New York. In his memory, I'm thinking of starting a Jack Scott scholarship."

"For somebody who wants to be a talk-show host," McCue whispered to me.

"And I'll talk to you all about that more as my plans crystallize," Birnbaum said. "Now, here's Sheriff Tillis."

"All's I want to do is find out how this accident happened," the sheriff said. "So I want to talk to you one at a time. I'd appreciate it if you just stay around the hotel or the dining room here so that you're nearby when I need you." He looked around and chuckled. "Heh, heh. Don't want to have to send no sheriff's posse after you. Might think you was trying to escape." He chuckled again, then looked at Birnbaum. "And count on it, Mr. Biffbaum, you can put the name of Sheriff Len Tillis down for a donation to that Jack Scott scholarship. Mark me down for ten dollars."

"Jesus, is this guy for real?" McCue asked me.

"He gets worse," I said.

An ambulance came and went with Scott's body as the sheriff questioned everybody who was staying in the hotel. At Snapp's suggestion, he let me sit in on the questioning.

"Never can tell, Len. He might help."

"I doubt it, Mr. Snapp, but for you, I'll give it a try."

The Hollywood people drifted in and out of the dining room as Tillis questioned them. I filled my glass a half-dozen times because what Tillis may have lacked in intelligence, he made up for in tenacity, asking the same questions over and over again, making voluminous word-for-word notes on an old writing tablet provided by Snapp.

It was late in the afternoon when Pamela Scott entered the dining room, wearing a black dress and dark sunglasses.

The sheriff was understanding. "I don't have to talk to you now, ma'am, if you'd rather wait."

"No, no. I'm all right now. It might help me to talk."

"Could you tell us then about last night, Mrs. Scott?"

"After we left dinner here, Jack and I went back to our room and talked for a while. We were planning to go back to New York today. Jack had some business that he wanted to take care of."

"What kind of business?" I asked.

"I don't know. He didn't say, but I thought I'd go back with him and spend the day with friends before coming back up here for the start of filming. At any rate, we talked some last night and then about nine o'clock, Jack got a phone call and said he was going out for a walk."

"Was your husband drinking?" the sheriff asked.

"Drinking? No, not Jack. Jack's habit was to have one drink a night before bed." She paused and looked away, as if trying to peer into the past. "A lot of ice, a little rye, and a lot of club soda. Jack was not a drinking man."

Tillis nodded. "And then?" he said.

"I took a shower and went to bed. It was kind of fun, reading by candlelight. I haven't done that since I was a Girl Scout. Then I went outside to get a book from the car and I saw that the tire was flat, so I asked Mr. Snapp to fix it. Then it seemed like a nice night and I went for a walk on the grounds. I met Mr. Tracy there."

"You didn't tell me that, Tracy," the sheriff said.

"It didn't come up," I said.

"And we walked back to the hotel together. What time would you say it was?"

"I remember looking at my watch. It was almost midnight," I said. Tillis was scribbling furiously in his notebook.

"Mr. Tracy walked me to my door. I went inside, but Jack wasn't there. I took a light sleeping pill. A Dalmane. I have insomnia, but Dalmane seems to work without aftereffects. I read a little more and fell alseep pretty quickly. Then I was awakened this morning by Biff and Mr. Tracy." She looked painfully shy, sorry at not being able to help more, and then shrugged. "That's all I know, Sheriff. Do you have any ideas about Jack's death?"

"That girl, what's her name, Sheila, said she talked to your husband about business at about nine o'clock," Tillis said. "A little after that, the Fluff woman saw him walking upstairs from your floor. But he didn't go to anyone's room up there."

"Where would he have gone, then?" she asked.

"Maybe he was looking out the window or something for the view," Tillis said. "But that was the last we know of his movements until we found the corpse . . . sorry, the body."

"A terrible accident. My poor Jack," she said as she rose. "I have to go back to my room now, Sheriff. If you don't mind."

"No. Go ahead, Mrs. Scott."

After she left, I said, "Well, Sheriff, what do you think?"

"I don't know. If he was a drinker, it'd be easy. He got blotto and got hung up fooling around with the rope. But how an accident like that happens to a sober man, I don't know. I guess it'll just be a mystery."

If it *was* an accident, I thought.

Sheila Hallowitz was sitting on the front steps of the hotel, drinking coffee, looking like a lost waif.

I sat down next to her and said, "I think we should talk."

"Sure. About what?"

"I didn't say anything when you were talking to the sheriff, but I think you ought to be a little more forthcoming right now."

"Forthcoming?"

"Dammit, Sheila, don't be cute with me. You told the sheriff that you were talking to Scott last night on the grounds, technical stuff about the film."

"Yes. That's true."

"Did you and Scott always talk by yelling at each other?" I asked.

She looked startled and I said, "I was watching. He was screaming at you. You were screaming back. Now I want to know what the hell that was all about."

Sheila looked off toward the horizon. Then she sipped her coffee. I was about to prod her when she said, "Jack was unhappy about our expenses. He said he wanted to discuss them with me."

"What expenses? How unhappy?" I asked.

"He thought I was going a lot over budget in these early stages. He wanted me to do an accounting."

"And he yelled at you about that? Seems sort of an ordinary thing to me," I said. "Why'd he yell?"

"I don't know," she said. "He seemed really worked up, but I don't know if he really was or if it was theater. A lot of men do that to women, you know. They yell, figuring they can browbeat us."

"You were yelling back," I said. "Why?"

"He wanted an accounting now. I asked him how I could do an accounting here when the offices are in Los Angeles. I told him I'd get it done as soon as I could, but it wasn't going to be next week or even the week after. I'd do it when I got to it."

"Why didn't you tell the sheriff about the argument?"

She looked at me with an earnest look in her eyes. "He wouldn't have understood," she said. "This kind of thing goes on all the time." She pressed her lips together in a tight line. "And, you know, I've talked to the other people around here, and if I told the sheriff we had argued, I might have been a suspect. I was the last person to see Jack Scott alive."

"No, you weren't," I said.

She looked at me quizzically.

"You're the last one who *admits* seeing Jack Scott alive," I said.

Sheriff Tillis was talking to Clyde Snapp near what would have been the front desk if the hotel were still a public operation.

"Len was just saying he heard from the hospital. The medical examiner said it was a broken neck that killed Scott," Snapp said.

"Time to close this one up," the sheriff said.

"Still a lot of questions unanswered," I said.

"Like what?"

"Like where was Scott last night after he left his room?"

"Hanging from that dumbwaiter rope, I guess," the sheriff said smugly.

I shook my head. "He left his room maybe around nine o'clock. His wife was still in the room. Then about eleven or a little after, she went out for a walk and came back near midnight. Scott still wasn't in the room. So where was he?"

"The way I figure it is he was off someplace drinking by himself. Then maybe when his wife went out, he came back. She wasn't there and he was drunk and he opened the dumbwaiter door and got himself hooked up and died, and when she came back, she didn't even know about it."

"He had the good sense, I guess, to close the dumb-waiter door after himself," I said sarcastically, "so his dead body didn't disturb his wife when she came back from her walk."

"Listen, Mr. Private Detective. You can try to make things as complicated as you want, but that's the way it was and that's the way it's going to stay. You probably think I don't know anything about this kind of work, but I've been doing it a lot longer than you have. There's only three other entrances into that dumbwaiter. One is in the kitchen, but Clyde was down there all last night. The other two are in that Birnbaum's room, right over Scott's, and in McCue's room on the top floor. I looked at those doors and they were both screwed shut, the way Clyde fixed them. I don't know when Scott went through his own door in the dumbwaiter, but that's what he did. And then he died. Case closed. Now maybe you fancy private eyes can figure out something else, but us working cops can't."

"No criticism intended, Sheriff," I said. "You did a good job, especially questioning those people inside."

"It's my job, Tracy, and I do it every day."

"Don't the state police usually come in on a case like this one?" I asked.

"They come in to help if it's a murder or like that, and I told them this wasn't. Or else they come in to pester you and get their pictures in the paper. State police are good for getting their pictures in the paper."

He turned to Clyde. "Well, Mr. Snapp, I think I'm about done here. I'd better get a move on. The missus is going to be sore anyway 'cause I was supposed to paint the garage today." He held up his notepad. "And I'm not done yet. A lot of typing to do before I'm done tonight."

The telephone behind the front desk rang with a curious buzzing sound. Snapp picked it up, listened for a moment, and said, "Don't let anybody in. That's an order." He leaned over the counter to put the handset back on the base.

"There's some television guys outside," he told me. "I told Jerry at the gate to keep them out."

"Good," I said.

"I'm leaving anyway. I'll talk to them on my way out," Sheriff Tillis said. He started for the door and I thought it was best to let Birnbaum know that the press wolves had arrived.

Naturally, he was in his room, lifting weights.

"Some press people have arrived. The sheriff just went out to talk to them."

"Jesus Christ," he said. "Just what we need. Gomer Pyle explains the world." He grabbed his Mets jacket off the back of a chair. "I'd better do what I can to salvage this."

"Was he on drugs? Was this a drug-related death?"

"How the hell would I know if he was on drugs?" Sheriff Tillis answered back. He was standing alongside his car just outside the front gate, facing four men and a woman. The woman and one man seemed to be reporters because they were wearing neat clothing, suitable for filming. The other three men carried small video cameras. They looked like hair balls, which was even more proof that they were photographers than the cameras they were carrying.

"You're the sheriff, aren't you? Aren't you supposed to know things like that?" the male reporter asked.

"That's right. And what I know is that we had an accident and Mr. Scott died."

"But he was on drugs, right?" the woman reporter asked. "Or are you covering up the fact that he was on drugs?"

"Honey," the sheriff said, and she bristled. No one had been permitted to call her "honey" since her father had. No one had wanted to either, I'd bet. "I don't know anything about any drugs, honey," the sheriff said. "And the coroner didn't say anything about them, so I think maybe you're the one on drugs." He smiled at her and I thought, Three cheers for Sheriff Tillis.

Birnbaum stepped up to the closed gate.

"Folks, I'm Biff Birnbaum, producer of *Corridors of Death*. If you will be patient, we'll have a statement for you in a little while."

The five newspeople abandoned Sheriff Tillis and flocked toward the closed fence. Tillis looked at me and I winked and he smiled back.

"Was Scott a heavy drug-user, or just a recreational drug-user?" the male reporter asked.

"Jack Scott was my partner for ten years. He never took a drug in his life."

"He was a drunk, though, right?" the woman reporter said. "Everybody knew he was a drunk."

"I don't know who you've been talking to miss, but your information is wrong. Everybody who knew Jack Scott knew he did not drink. Please. Hold your questions. I'll have a statement very soon."

"Who's in there? Is Tony McCue in there?" the woman asked.

"I don't know where Tony McCue is," Birnbaum said. I thought maybe he went to a Jesuit college too because it was a neat mental reservation of the first order.

"Who *is* in there?"

"Yeah. Who?"

"I'll have a statement shortly," Birnbaum said. He turned to the guard. "Please keep this gate locked and let no one in."

"Mr. Snapp told me that already," the guard said.

"We're the press. We have a right to be in there. You

don't have any right to keep us out," the woman reporter yelled.

"Is Mrs. Scott in there?" the man yelled at Birnbaum.
"I want to talk to Mrs. Scott. Send her out here."

"I'll provide a statement in a little while," Birnbaum
said.

"What kind of a name is Biff Birnbaum anyway?" the
woman reporter sneered. "You sound like a porn
producer."

"A statement soon," Birnbaum said as he walked
away.

The sheriff drove off and the guard moved over to
stand in front of the closed gate.

"Who are you?" the woman yelled at me through the
iron bars.

"My name is Devlin Tracy."

"Who are you with?"

"Nobody," I said.

"What's your name again?" the male reporter repeated.

"Devlin Tracy."

"I never heard of you," the woman reporter shouted.

"Too bad," I said. "I've heard of *you* in every football
locker room from here to Los Angeles."

I walked away. Behind me, I could hear the two
reporters screaming.

"We want McCue."

"We want Mrs. Scott."

"First amendment."

"Censorship."

"Let us in."

I wondered if sometimes the cameramen were embarrassed by the low caliber of the people they had to work
with.

28

The crowd of reporters and cameramen outside the gate had swelled, and Clyde Snapp had put an extra guard on duty patrolling the grounds to make sure nobody sneaked in.

I was watching them through the lobby window, and the mob scene, now grown to about twenty, reminded me of some band of rabble demonstrating outside the gates of an American embassy somewhere. The barbarians versus civilization. It was real strange. Only when stacked up against the press could these Hollywood types I was with be representing "civilization."

Tony McCue came to stand alongside me.

"Listen to them," I said. "You're a big hit out here in the sticks."

He cracked the front door a few inches, and the sound of the gentlemen and ladies of the media drifted in.

"We want McCue."

"Send out McCue."

"Where's Tony McCue?"

He let the door swing closed and looked at me with a shrug.

"I guess they weren't satisfied with Birnbaum's statement," I said.

"What'd he say?"

"He said that there was a tragic accident, that one of America's most beloved entertainment figures had died, that specific information on the accident would have to come from the police, that he planned to go ahead with this film as a monument to a great entertainer. He made some reference to Scott's clean personal life—no drugs, no alcohol—and to their long friendship."

"The part about drinking's true enough," McCue said. "The little shit didn't even enjoy taking a drink."

"And Birnbaum told them that his wife was under sedation and would make no statements until she returned to their home in New York City and everyone here would appreciate it if they would please leave and show some consideration for the grieving widow."

"And what'd they say?"

"One of them said, 'Fuck you, Birnbaum.' "

"It's amazing how the media can ruin even the best of times," McCue said.

"Best of times? You know, Tony, you don't seem real broken up about Scott's death."

"Come on, Trace. What's one producer more or less? They're fools and thieves. And there are new fools and thieves standing ten deep to replace him. The only creatures worse in the world are these bastards of the press. Do you know that for four years they have been dogging my footsteps wherever I go, rooting through my garbage, disguising themselves as waiters in restaurants so they can listen in to table talk. They bribed a maid of mine once to tell them about my sex life."

"They must have run that article as a series," I said. "What'd she tell them?"

"That I screwed her and gave her plane fare back to Puerto Rico."

"Was it true?"

"Yes. She was lousy in bed. Who needs that kind of maid? I gave the employment agency hell."

He pushed open the door again and listened to the reporters, who were still shouting. Then he walked inside the dining room and came out with a paper bar napkin that he stuck into his pocket.

"I think it is entirely appropriate that I should talk to the press," he told me. "After all, *le cinéma c'est moi.*"

I followed him outside. He put on his reading glasses as he approached the gate, and the reporters cheered his approach.

"Statement."

"Who supplied Scott with the drugs, McCue?"

"Isn't it true he died after an all-night drinking bout with you?"

"Tell the truth, McCue."

"How much responsibility do you feel for causing his death, McCue?"

McCue stayed inside the gate and raised a hand for silence.

"All in good time," he said. "I have a statement."

He took the bar napkin from his pocket.

"I'd like to read this," he said. "Are you ready?"

The reporters all shouted at once and McCue shouted back, "Will you hold it down so I can read this? I'm reading it only once."

The reporters grumbled but started to quiet down.

Using his deepest, most sober voice, McCue looked down and pretended to read from his cocktail napkin.

"Ladies and gentlemen of the press." He stopped for a moment and looked up. "Are all those cameras running? I'm not repeating this."

"Yeah, yeah, go ahead, McCue, go ahead."

"All right." He cleared his throat and pushed his eyeglasses farther down his nose.

"Ladies and gentlemen of the press, I have been asked to comment on the tragic death of Jack Scott. My only comment is this: you people of the media are a disgusting batch of assholes. You are fucking vampires. If I had children who wanted to be reporters, I would send them out on the street to give blowjobs instead. America would be a richer country if it repealed the first amendment and threw all of you motherfuckers into concentration camps. You are shit. Your reports are shit. Your brains are shit. You may all go fuck yourselves."

He stuck the napkin back into his pocket, took off his reading glasses, and said, "That concludes my statement. I will take no questions."

He started back to the hotel. I walked along with him. The reporters were screeching behind us.

"I've always wanted to do that," he said. "I just hope it was live on some of the channels."

"I hope so too," I said. "McCue, I'm proud to know you. Come on. I'll build you a drink."

"You're on."

Naturally, Walter Marks wound up ruining the day by calling me. I thought he was going to congratulate me for keeping McCue alive. I should have known better.

"Why is it, Trace, that wherever you go, there's trouble?"

"Just lucky, I guess," I said. "Anything else?"

"Not so fast. So what happened to Scott? Was it really an accident like the television's saying?"

"I don't know."

"Is there a mad killer running loose up there?"

"I don't know."

"What do you know?" he snapped.

"I know that you're paying me five hundred dollars a day plus expenses, but if you're going to keep calling me all the time, I'm going to raise the fee."

"Not a chance. And you just keep an eye on that McCue. The television said he was not cooperative with the reporters. Was he drinking?"

"I thought he was very forthright and open with them. And he's drinking like he always drinks, like a freaking fish."

"You watch him, Trace. Don't let anything happen to him. Six million dollars is a lot of money."

"And on that highly informative note, I'll say good night. Good night, Groucho."

After I hung up, I tried Chico, but there was no answer. And Sarge didn't answer either. So I went to bed.

McCue was snoring next door. God's in his heaven, all's right with the world.

29

In their own way, showers are pretty neat things. If you take one at night, it helps you sleep. If you take one in the morning, it helps you wake up. I don't know what would happen if you took one, say, at two P.M., and I'm going to have to find out.

I thought maybe I'd ask Chico when I saw her; that woman knows everything.

Anyway, I was thinking of that, and it reminded me of the old joke about the guy who tells an interviewer that the greatest scientific invention of all time was the thermos bottle. He was asked why and he said because it keeps the hot food hot and the cold food cold.

"What's so big deal about that?" the interviewer asked.

"How does it know?" the man said.

Same thing with showers.

Anyway, I took a shower and fell right to sleep, but it was troubled sleep, and that was unusual for me. Troubled sleep is for people who worry about what they're doing, who care about what other people think. I didn't have any of those problems, but I kept waking up in the middle of the night, mind chewing over the death of Jack Scott.

I'd wake up, think for a moment in the twilight of my semi-sleeping brain, and then doze off again.

I wondered why Jack Scott would be fooling around with a dumbwaiter rope. Was it possible that he just fell into the dumbwaiter shaft by accident and the rope incredibly twisted around his neck? But why the hell did he open the door in the first place? Or did someone else unlock it?

And another time, I woke up and thought, Suppose Scott has been murdered. Why Scott? Tony McCue was the one whose medicines had been spilled out; Tony McCue was the one on whose head the large rock almost fell.

And then I woke up again later and thought, Maybe not. Maybe the rock was meant to kill Roddy Quine. Maybe there had been three murder attempts and only one successful. Could that be so? But what about the hit-and-run?

Later I thought, maybe somebody wanted to kill anybody, somebody, everybody, a lot of people. Who, though? Everybody here hated somebody else, but I didn't think somebody hated everybody. Who would have anything to gain by multiple killings?

Then I thought about the hotel. Was it possible? The owner of the place had rented it to the movie company for a whistle, somebody said. Just for the publicity, which would help him reopen the place and make a buck out of it.

Who was that owner? Had he thought of a really wonderful way to get publicity? By killing people? It had already worked. The press goons had spent the whole day and night standing outside the front gate of the Canestoga Hotel.

I decided that in the morning I'd have to find out

something about the owner of the hotel. And I'd have to talk to Sheila Hallowitz again because I didn't believe for a minute that she and Scott had gone out into the grounds of the hotel during a rainstorm so that they could discuss a budget.

I fell back asleep. Then another disturbance.

I thought I felt someone crawling into bed with me.

I did. There was someone under the covers. I was awake now and I felt a hand touch me.

I should have locked the door. Why did I always forget to lock doors?

I felt a soft feminine hand touch me under the sheet.

"I told you, I've gone straight," I mumbled.

The hand stroked me more insistently.

"Thank you," I said, "but you've got to go now. I'm bespoken."

The first hand was joined by a second hand, which did nice things to my stomach. I grabbed both hands, pulled them outside the sheet, and pushed them away.

"My girlfriend wouldn't like that," I said. "Now get out of here before I call the police."

A soft voice whispered in the air with an accent borrowed from Zsa Zsa Gabor.

"Don't you like me, dollink?"

"I'll like you better when you leave."

"Vell, dollink. I'm not leavink, not ever."

I sighed loud. "Okay," I said, and rolled over on top of the woman next to me.

"You prick," the voice said. No accent this time.

"Why, Chico. What a surprise."

"I'll bet it was a surprise. I'll bet you never expected it was going to be my bones you were jumping on. Get off me, you huge philandering cretin, you."

I reached over, turned on the light, then propped myself over her on extended arms.

"Why are you smiling?" she said.

"Just surprised to see you. When did you arrive?"

"Screw arrive. I'm leaving," she said. "Let me out of here."

Her pretty bow's mouth was fixed in a scowl. Her sloe eyes were narrowed, the dark pupils glinting in the harsh bed lamp's light. She looked at me and then slowly her expression softened.

"How'd you know it was me?" she said.

"I didn't until you started doing Zsa Zsa Gabor. You do the lousiest Zsa Zsa I ever heard."

"Oh, aren't you nice?" she said. "When you thought I was somebody else, you were going to chase me away. Now that's loyalty for you. Trace, I'm impressed."

I rolled over onto my back. "Not really," I said. "I thought you were that goddamn queen, Roddy Quine. Now, if you had been one of the thousands of beautiful chickies who are running around here half-naked all the time, it might have been a different story."

"Who? What beautiful chickies?"

"Let's see." I stretched it out as I lit a cigarette. "There's Blow-blow La Flume. She's the production coordinator on this opus. And then there's . . . Oh, bullshit. When'd you arrive? What are you doing here?"

"I heard on the news about Scott's death, so I figured, Screw the packing, it'll wait, and I lucked up and caught a plane right away and came here. Is it murder?"

"I don't know."

"Do you have an extra gun for me? In case it is?"

"I don't even have one for myself. Did you talk to Sarge?"

"Yes. He told me my gun permit arrived. I still think you lied and tried to hide it."

"Why do you think that ridiculous thing?" I asked.

" 'Cause Sarge told me that you did."

"The uncorroborated testimony of an accomplice won't stand up in court," I said.

"It won't go to court. So you don't have a gun?"

"No," I said.

"That's all right. I'll buy one tomorrow."

"I figured you'd have one by now. How'd you get past the guard at the gate if you didn't shoot your way in?"

"The guard's not too bright. I razzle-dazzled him with my business cards."

"The ones that say 'Chico Mangini and Friends, Private Investigators?'" I asked.

"Yes."

"Well, I'm glad you're here. Take off your clothes and stay awhile."

"I'll do both. You tell me what's going on. I want something to drink. You have a refrigerator?"

"No."

"These old hotels always have refrigerators," she said.

"Sorry, babe. I don't have one."

"I bet everybody else has got a refrigerator."

"Did you come up here to harp on the lack of respect shown me?" I asked.

"No. I came up here to show you what a lack of respect really is. What the hell is that ghastly noise?"

"Your first encounter with a star," I said. "That's Tony McCue snoring." I jerked my thumb toward the wall behind the bed.

"We'll straighten *that* out tomorrow," she said. She bounded out of bed. She was wearing a white skirt, cut short to show off her really marvelous legs, some kind of dark-blue striped blouse, and a pink jacket of soft leather.

A leather garment bag lay on the floor, next to one of those gigantic pocketbooks that women always seem to carry just to make sure they can never find their keys when they need them.

She rooted around inside the purse for a few moments, then came out with a can of ginger ale and a sandwich in plastic wrap.

"*Voilà*," she exclaimed.

"Congratulations. Mealtime's not for a couple of hours yet. I don't know how you would have survived."

Without moving from the spot where she was standing, she ripped open the plastic wrap around the sandwich and took a large bite. "Ham and cheese," she said. "I love ham-and-cheese sandwiches." She was talking with her mouth full.

"Hey, save that for the tourists," I said. "I've seen you eat. If you were hungry, you'd love grasshopper-and-grub chips."

"Food is the music of love, and I do believe in playing on," she mumbled. The sandwich was already half-gone.

She took a big swallow, a sip of soda, and said, "I haven't eaten since my plane landed at Ithaca. What's been going on? Why didn't you bring the tape recorder?"

"First of all, I didn't expect anybody to die on me here. And second of all, I don't want to keep being a slave to the tape recorder. If you're going to make me work for Sarge's agency, I'm going to do it my way. No tape recorders. This is the new me."

The rest of the sandwich vanished inside her mouth. One more swallow and it would only be a memory. I once saw a snake ingesting a frog in the San Diego Zoo. This was the same. She gulped.

"You should use your tape recorder all the time. Trace, you haven't any memory."

"Sorry. I forgot."

"Tell me about Scott and who's here and all."

"Only if you come to bed," I said.

"You first."

So I started recounting the events of the last two days and the cast of characters at the hotel. It was not an easy job because I kept getting distracted as Chico, between sips of her ginger ale, started to remove her clothes, one slow garment at one slow time.

"Why are you stopping?" she said.

"How the hell do you expect me to concentrate when you're doing a striptease?"

"I didn't think I affected you anymore," she said.

"I'll let you know when you don't. Now get your clothes off and get into bed if you want me to finish my story."

"All right, if that's the price I've got to pay."

"That's only part of the price," I said.

"As my favorite writer says, 'Nothing is more unbooted than blab, more nowhere than hustle,'" she said. She took off all her clothes. Most women need clothes to cover their flaws. Chico has no flaws. Naked, beautiful, she padded around the room, carefully hanging her clothes up in the unused closet.

"I can see you've done your usual dresser-drawer number with your clothes," she said. "Don't you ever unpack?"

"I didn't unpack them in New York. I didn't see any reason to unpack them here. When they're all dirty and I get them cleaned, then maybe I'll hang them up."

"Or when the board of health comes for you, whichever occurs first." She slid under the sheet next to me and said, "You come here often, big boy?" and snapped imaginary gum at me.

"Now that you're here, I would hope so," I said. I rolled on my side and kissed her. "Hello."

"Good-bye. Tell me first what's going on."

Once Chico gets an idea in her head, there is no deflecting her. I lit another cigarette, lay back, and continued the two-day report. I tried to leave nothing out, not even Tami Fluff coming on to me.

"Bitch," she said.

"Come on. You can't blame the poor girl, can you?"

"Can't blame her? First she sneaks into McCue's room to do boom-boom, then the next afternoon, she's after you. She ought to have a governor installed on her crotch. I'll bet that was her I saw when I arrived here."

"What her? Who?"

"I saw two people out alongside the hotel, on the grounds. They were walking together. It looked very sexual."

"How does walking look sexual?"

"If you don't know, I can't tell you."

"Who were they?" I said.

"I don't know. I don't know anybody here yet and I couldn't see them real well. It was probably Tami Fluff. Probably picked up a sailor somewhere."

"If you're going to be narrow-minded, I'm sorry I told you."

"That's it. Take her side. Go on with your stupid story."

I plugged along until I thought I was finally done, but she quickly disabused me of that.

"You have done some piss-poor job," she said.

"Hey, babe. McCue's still alive. If you listen, you can hear him snoring. That's what I'm paid to do. I did it. Get off my case."

"So *was* there anything funny in the pills in his room?"

"I don't know."

"See? That's what I mean," Chico said. "Piss-poor. If you don't find out if there was anything in the pills, how can you know if somebody was trying to kill him? Hah? How?"

I sighed. "I thought I would just wait for you to arrive and straighten it all out for me."

"Then I'm here just in time," she said. "Go to sleep."

"I want to fool around," I said.

"I want to think. Go to sleep."

"Think while we're fooling around," I said.

"Go to sleep. I'll wake you when I'm done thinking."

"That better be a promise," I said.

I went to sleep and she woke me up.

"You done thinking already?"

"No. Did Scott have anything on him when you found his body?"

"I don't think so. I don't know. Nothing like a gun, though. The sheriff would have said something about that."

"Damn."

"There was water in the dumbwaiter shaft," I said.

"What kind of water?"

"The usual kind. Wet, colorless, the kind that wets the knees of your pants. And a plastic container."

"What kind of container?"

"Damn it, I don't want to answer questions. I want to trick."

"What kind of a container?" Chico asked.

"Plastic. Like a margarine container. Something like that."

"What was in it?"

"Nothing. It was empty," I said.

"Was it wet?"

"I don't know."

"Where's the container now?" she asked.

This woman was turning into a large pain in the ass.

"I don't know where the container is now. Probably in the garbage," I said. "Can I go back to sleep now?"

"Yes. No. Wait. You say Birnbaum's room is on top of Scott's?"

"Right. And McCue's is still farther on top."

"Come on, Trace. Get up," she said.

"I thought I'd never hear that. I'm already up."

She jumped out of bed. "Hold that thought," she said, "while you put some clothes on."

"Go to hell," I said.

She grabbed my foot and pulled me out of bed.

"In the morning, I'm going to find out when the next plane goes back to Vegas," I said.

30

The basement kitchen was dark when we walked in, so I struck a match. But I didn't get a chance to enjoy it because an arm grabbed me around the throat, pressing hard against my windpipe.

"Don't move, fella," the voice said.

I croaked a little bit. "Clyde. It's me, Trace. Let up."

The overhead fluorescent lights flashed on and I blinked my eyes as the pressure on my neck was released.

"Sorry, Tracy," Snapp said. He walked around in front of me. "Just taking no chances, I guess." He saw Chico standing in the doorway. "Who's this?"

"My associate, Chico."

"You're lucky I didn't bring my gun," she told Clyde. "You would have had a slug in your guts."

"Don't pay any attention to her," I said. "She just talks that way."

"Still and all, I *ain't* gonna get her mad," Snapp said.

He was wearing pajamas. It was the first time I'd seen him in anything but his gray whipcord pants and plaid shirt.

"So what can I do for you?" he asked me.

"Ask her."

"Did you throw out today's garbage yet?" Chico said.

"Huh?"

"Today's garbage. Did you throw it out?"

"No. It's over there." Clyde waved an arm in the general direction of the other end of the kitchen. "Are you interested in any special garbage or just garbage in general?"

"I'm interested in that plastic container you took out of the dumbwaiter shaft."

"It's in the bag," he said.

"Do you remember?" Chico asked. "Was it wet?"

"Wet? I got to think. Yeah, I guess it was a little wet."

"Good."

"Good," Snapp repeated. "See, Tracy? It's good that it was wet."

"Don't worry," I said. "She always makes it make sense in the last chapter."

Chico went over to the side of the stainless-steel table, where a large green plastic garbage bag was puffed up full with waste.

She opened the top of the bag. "Uggggh," she said. "What a mess. Trace."

"Not me, pal. You're on your own. It's your dumb idea."

"Tricking along together," she began to sing.

"All right. Blackmailer," I said.

She handed me a fresh hefty bag. "I just want you to hold," she said. She asked Clyde, "This is tonight's dinner garbage?"

"Aaay-p," he said. He went over and sat on his cot to watch. I guess he didn't get much chance to see garbage-pickers in action.

Chico had put on jeans and a sweatshirt; she pushed her sleeves back and with no visible sign of distaste plunged both her hands into the garbage bag. For a moment I thought she was going to eat her way through it, but no, she pulled up a handful and dropped it into the open top of the bag I was holding.

She kept that up, bringing out sodden handfuls of food, dropping them in the open bag, and I was just glad, all of a sudden, that Clyde hadn't decided to cook chicken à la king for dinner.

"This is disgusting," I said.

"Hey. I'm doing the disgusting part," she said. "Just hold the bag."

Halfway down in the garbage bag, she came across a plastic margarine tub, one of the large two-pound sizes.

"This it?" she asked.

"I think so," I said.

"That's it," Snapp said.

The tub was filled with paper towels and Chico took them out.

I said, "Hold it. Those were the towels Clyde used to blot up the water."

"Good," she said.

"She put the plastic container on the table, wiped its outside with a clean paper towel, and told me, "Tie up those bags, will you?"

She went to the sink and washed her arms and hands under the running water while I rewrapped garbage.

Snapp said to her, "It's time for the septic tank to be flushed. Don't suppose you'd be interested, would you?"

"Depends on what it pays," she said. She scrambled lightly, like the dancer she was, up onto the stainless-steel-topped table. "This is the dumbwaiter shaft?" she said.

"Yeah. Scott's suite is right above it."

"Mr. Snapp, have you got a flashlight?"

"Sure, little girl," he said. "People have a habit of calling Chico "little woman" or "little girl." I think this is because she's little, but somehow she thinks it's because men are disgusting sexist pigs who should all be castrated, the sooner the better. Generally, I don't agree with that position.

He handed her the light and said, "You really a detective?"

"Aaaay-p," she said.

"Are you detecting now?" Clyde asked.

"Yes."

"Detect anything yet?" he asked.

"I don't know," she said. "I think so." She stood up inside the dumbwaiter shaft. Only her legs from about midthigh were visible.

I noticed that she was wearing white leather running shoes, and by God, she even managed to look sexy in sneakers.

She squatted down and stuck her head out of the shaft. "Three doors up there. That's Scott, Birnbaum, and McCue, right?"

"Right," Snapp said. "This shaft services all those rooms, but it's not in service anymore."

"All right," she said, and disappeared into the shaft again. "God, this is dusty," she said softly.

"You mean you're traveling without your killer wash rag?" I said.

"Be quiet," she hissed back.

I finished sealing the two garbage bags, pushed them into a corner, and shrugged toward Snapp, who was monitoring Chico's progress with a bemused expression on his face. I had forgotten my cigarettes, so I took a pack out of the tall cupboard and lit it from the gas stove.

Chico finally came out of the shaft and closed the door behind her. "The rope was wrapped around Scott's neck?" she asked.

I nodded. "Once around."

"That rope's strung real tight," she said. "How'd you get him out? There's no play in the rope."

"Sheriff Tillis is this guy who looks like Gorilla Monsoon," I said. "He reached up and rassled around and untwisted it from his neck."

"Does this all mean something?" Snapp asked.

"It means I'm going to sleep," Chico said. "I'm really tired."

"At last," I said.

Chico said, "Mr. Snapp, how early do you think you could call the sheriff? You know him, right?"

"It's Sunday. Maybe seven, seven-thirty."

"Good. I'll be down around then. We can talk to him."

"I look forward to it, little girl. Should I save any garbage or anything for you?"

"No. Just don't let anyone mess with the dumbwaiter," she said. She took the margarine container and started for the door. Then she stopped and went back to the large commercial refrigerator in the center of the kitchen, took a piece of Danish from inside, and left the room chomping happily.

31

Chico was under the sheet, astride my body, when I woke up. It's one of my six favorite ways to wake up. The other five also involve Chico, but they require marching bands, prothonotary warblers, sixteen cases of pressurized whipped cream, and the roof from the Astrodome, so they're kind of hard to put together at a moment's notice.

"Yankee soldier want to play around?"

"No. I've had so much fun in the last six months, I've decided to remain celibate for the rest of my life."

"Okay," she said brightly, and turned to spring out of bed. "Breakfast is ready anyway."

I grabbed her wrist and pulled her to me. "Get back here, you half-breed savage."

She sighed and rolled her eyes. "Okay, but make it fast, will you, ace? I don't want to miss breakfast."

"Wait. Weren't you supposed to see Clyde this morning?"

"I did. That's how I know breakfast is ready. I helped him cook. He's an awful cook."

"If you helped him cook, then I know you're not hungry. I've seen you cook."

"You've found me out, big fella. Do with me what you will," she said.

"You know what you're letting yourself in for, don't you?"

"Oh, no, not that. Not that."

"That's right," I said. "The dreaded Himalayan Highway Hump."

Halfway along, I said to Chico, "The nice thing about sex is that it's like riding a bicycle. You never forget how."

"Pedal faster," she said.

When we were done, we showered together, which raised a new problem to which we found a solution right in the bathtub. We then went down to breakfast, even though by that time, I'd rather have gone back to bed. Sometimes showers *don't* know.

Chico apparently had some pride of authorship in what she had helped Clyde cook for breakfast, because she had a double helping of everything and then went back for more and came back balancing two plates, one of them for me.

She brought me the plate because she is, after all, both my consort and a lady.

A. She hoped I would eat something if it was placed in front of me and usually I would pick a little bit.

B. More important, what I didn't eat, she would, and that way she could have three plates full without anyone seeing her go through the food line three times. As she told me once, it helps to plan ahead.

Birnbaum, Sheila, and Roddy Quine were at the table in the far corner when we arrived. Sheila and Birnbaum had nodded toward me, but Roddy Quine did not acknowledge our presence.

Birnbaum walked quickly past our table. He was wearing a jogging suit.

"Who's that?" Chico asked with her mouth full.

"That's Birnbaum," I said. "He must have bad kidneys because he's always on the run out of the dining room."

"Maybe," she said.

She had finished her plate and was halfway through mine when Birnbaum came back to the room, now wearing his Mets jacket. He plopped down at our table.

"They're back, they're back," he said so quickly it sounded as if he were being charged for air time. "Those damned reporters are back."

"Probably forever," I said. I noticed Chico was giving him a close inspection.

"So introduce us," he said.

"This is my associate, Chico Mangini. This is Biff Birnbaum, the producer."

He shook her hand. He said how happy he was that she'd come to visit; he said everyone felt better now that she was there, and then, almost in midsentence it seemed, he jumped up and walked back to his own table.

"That's what I call a case of nerves," I said.

She held her right hand out before her and with her left index finger pointed to a white smudge of powder on her hand.

"Not nerves," she said. "And not bad kidneys either."

"What?"

She leaned forward and whispered. "He's a cokehead, Trace. He went out of here to go do a line." She tapped the powder on her hand again, then wiped it off with a napkin and kept eating.

Tony McCue wandered into the dining room, saw the two of us, came, sat down, and said to Chico, "Will you marry me?"

"No."

"Why not? I'm rich and famous," he said.

"You drink too much," she said.

"I'll bet he told you that," McCue said. "Do you know that since I've been here, I've done nothing but try to keep him sober."

"You did a lousy job," Chico said.

"Just the other night I had to pull him out of a barroom brawl before he got himself hurt. I'll bet he didn't tell you that."

"Not in so many words," Chico said.

Snapp walked over to our table and whispered something in Chico's ear.

She told me, "I'll be right back, Trace."

McCue rose as she left the table, making me feel self-conscious about my lousy manners. When he sat back down, he said, "She's not an actress, is she?"

"All women are actresses," I said.

"But does she make a living at it?"

"No. She's a detective."

"What a waste," he said.

"Tell me something I don't know," I said.

Ramona Dedley joined us at the table. She was wearing abbreviated shorts and a tight halter top. She and McCue were getting food when Chico returned.

She looked around as she sat down, and said, "Who's the bimbo with McCue?"

"Careful. That one's the shrink," I said.

"If analysis makes you look like that, I may sign up," she said.

"You don't need it."

McCue made elaborate introductions when they came back to the table, getting Chico's name right. Ramona did what women almost always do: she took the measure of Chico as possible opposition and decided that Chico won. That was a thing Chico never did: she never measured herself against others. Some might think it was because she was so arrogant she was sure she'd win, but the truth was that she didn't really care. For certain, I had never met any other woman in my life so quick to compliment another woman on her beauty.

We made small talk until Tony left for the men's room.

Chico said, "Doctor Dedley . . ."

"Ramona, please."

"Okay. Ramona, if Tony took potassium chloride, what would happen?"

"He'd probably die. Why?"

"Just bear with me a moment. How would that happen? Is it because he's taking digoxin?"

The doctor nodded. "Digoxin slows down the heart rate generally in a patient like Tony. You could say that it lets the chambers fill better and pump better. Now if you took potassium chloride at the same time, the two of them together would probably smother the heart. They could cause cardiac arrest."

"Is it easy to detect?" Chico asked.

Ramona shook her head. "A good forensic man could find it if he were looking for it. But chances are it would just slide by undetected. I have to ask you why?"

"Yeah. Why?" I said.

"I think those pills that Trace took out of Tony's room might have potassium chloride in them," Chico said.

"Oh, my God." Ramona shrugged her shoulders in irritation. "I haven't even had them analyzed yet."

"I've got a lab technician available," Chico said. She looked at me. "A friend of the sheriff's. He'll test them out for us right away."

"I'm going to my room and get them," Ramona said.

As she stood to leave, Pamela Scott entered the room, wearing the same black dress and sunglasses. Biff Birnbaum met her and walked with her to his table. She nodded at me as she walked by, and I saw Chico staring at the two of them.

"Mrs. Scott," I explained to her.

"Good," Chico said. She stood up and said, "I'll be right back." She grabbed her big purse from under her seat and walked quickly from the room. She was back in less than two minutes, with a quiet smile on her face.

"You look like you swallowed the canary," I said.

"Better than that," she said. She opened her purse on her lap and pointed inside. I looked.

"That looks like an ice-cube tray," I said.

"It is," she said.

"You're reduced now to carrying around your own ice-cube trays?" I said.

"Don't be a dork," she said. "It's not my ice-cube tray. For God's sakes, I'm staying with a man who doesn't even rate a refrigerator in his room. The shame of it all."

"Whose is it?"

"It came from Mrs. Scott's room," Chico said, and winked at me.

Ramona came back and handed Chico a small paper bag, which she dropped into the maw of her purse.

"All the drugs are labeled," Ramona said.

"Good." Chico said. "I'm going to give these to Clyde. He'll have one of his guards run them up to the hospital lab."

"The ice-cube tray too?" I said.

"Of course," she said. "That's the most important thing of all."

32

We went up to Tony McCue's top-floor suite after breakfast. Chico had borrowed Clyde Snapp's flashlight.

She walked over to inspect the dumbwaiter door.

"Trace, look at this," she said. "You told me this was locked, right?"

"Sure." I pulled on the small metal handle. "It's still locked."

"But look at the screw," she said. "The paint's chipped."

"So what?"

"So Clyde locked all these dumbwaiter doors by driving a screw into the frame. And then he painted over them when he painted the rooms. He told me that. Somebody has opened this door."

"I didn't do it," McCue said. He went to the refrigerator, took out a tray of ice cubes, emptied it into the ice bucket atop the refrigerator, and started to make himself a drink.

"I know you didn't," Chico said. She rooted around in her purse and came out with one of those things called a Swiss Army knife, which has scissors and screwdrivers and nail clippers. I always wondered how there could be a Swiss Army knife when there wasn't even a Swiss Army that I knew about.

She started removing the two-inch-long brass screw from next to the door handle. "See? Somebody opened it, and then put the screw back in later. When they opened it, they chipped the paint."

She opened the door into the dumbwaiter and leaned in with the flashlight.

"Ahhhh," she said. It was a purely animal sound of satisfaction and it occurred to me that it was a sound I didn't hear much from her. Maybe sex *wasn't* the same as riding a bicycle, but was it my fault I didn't get more practice? Going straight sucks.

"Look, Trace," Chico said.

I leaned in alongside her as Ramona walked up behind us. McCue was sitting on the windowsill, sipping his drink, looking out over the grounds, appearing bored with it all.

"Look at the pulley," Chico said softly. The pulley was about five feet above where our heads were, and Chico shined the light on it.

"Nice pulley," I said.

"Dimbulb," she whispered. "You see the rope on the other side of the pulley? It's coated with dust. But on this side, look." She shone the light on the rope, from the pulley, past our eye level, then down into the shaft. About fifteen feet of the rope had no dust on it.

"You see?" she said. "The rope's been moved. The dust was scraped off as it came through the pulley."

Ramona leaned over my shoulder to look. I felt her breasts against my back.

"So what?" I said to Chico. "Probably Jack Scott's weight pulled the rope down."

"No. There's a lock on the pulley down in the basement. You remember seeing it?"

"Yes. But maybe Scott's weight was enough to pull it down anyway."

"No, it wasn't," she said. "Look." She clambered up onto the shelf from the doorway to the dumbwaiter, crouched there, and handed me the flashlight. Then she put her hands on the dumbwaiter rope and let her body hang into the shaft.

"Careful, dammit," I said.

"Shhhh," she answered. She swung lightly back inside the room. "See? My weight didn't even move the rope and Scott was a little guy. His weight wouldn't have moved it either." She looked at Ramona. "You examined Scott's body, Ramona?"

Ramona nodded. "Yes. I don't understand."

"Think," Chico said. "Was there dust around his neck from the rope?"

I could see Ramona thinking, trying to recreate the moment when she had felt Scott's throat. "Yes," she said finally.

"I thought so," Chico said, and looked smug.

We heard a telephone ringing. By the time I realized it was the phone in my room, Chico was out the door. I looked at McCue and shrugged.

He said, "I hate it when women are smarter than me. Don't you?"

"I wouldn't know," I said. "I've never met a woman smarter than me."

For some reason, this prompted gales of laughter from Ramona Dedley. I didn't think it was that funny.

"Present company included," I said.

Ramona thought this was doubly hilarious. I didn't. I'm getting tired of people thinking I'm dumb, and I'm certainly not going to stay in a roomful of people who feel that way, so I walked over to my room just as Chico was hanging up the telephone.

"Walter Marks sends his love," she said.

"I send him a case of acne," I said. "Why are you talking to Groucho?"

"I asked him to find out something for us," she said.

"Did he?"

"Yes."

"What?" I asked.

"A motive for Jack Scott's murder," she said.

"Murder? You sure?"

"I think so," she said. "I'll know when I get a chance to get into some of these rooms."

Tony McCue had the telephone number of Biff Birnbaum's room and I called the producer.

"Birnbaum," he answered.

I dislike, on general principles, people who answer the telephone by reciting their name. I always say "hello." This is an example of my good manners and my total superiority to anyone who lives or works in California.

"This is Tracy. Is Sheila there?"

"Just a minute." I heard the phone being put down. This man had no telephone manners at all. I didn't ask to speak to Sheila. I just asked if she was there. He should have answered yes or no.

"Hello, Tracy," she said.

I said, "Let me talk to Birnbaum." I also said "please" because of my good manners, which everyone always compliments me on. Except Walter Marks' secretary. To hell with her. If they can't take a joke, fuck 'em.

Birnbaum said, "I thought you wanted to talk to Sheila."

"No. I just asked if she was there."

"Oh. Okay, now what?"

"I'm up in Tony McCue's room. Can you and Sheila come up here now and talk to us?"

"What about?"

"It's important," I said.

"All right," he said with a perceptible sigh. "We're coming right up."

McCue and Ramona sat on the sofa as I let the two of them in. Birnbaum was happy and smiling and I thought his Mets jacket ought to have a little Smile face on it. Sheila, though, looked worried.

"Hi, Tony. Ramona," Birnbaum said. He nodded to me. "What's up?" I was standing near the dumbwaiter door, which we had locked up again.

"I really wanted to talk to Sheila," I said, "but I thought you ought to be here."

"Okay," he said.

"I wanted to know what you were really talking about with Jack Scott Friday night on the grounds," I said to her.

"I told you. About the budget."

"I know that's what you told me. But now I'd like the truth."

"Hold on a minute," Birnbaum snapped. There was a sharp edge in his voice. "Are you calling Sheila a liar?"

I shrugged and Sheila said, "I told you the truth."

Behind me, through the dumbwaiter door, I could hear noises. That would be Chico working downstairs.

"Sheila," I said, "you don't go out in the middle of a storm to talk about a budget. You sit in your room or the dining room or someplace like that. Mrs. Scott told the sheriff that Jack had to go out and talk to you. That was right after he got a phone call from you. But you told me that he was the one who wanted to talk to you, not vice versa. Come on, Sheila. Let's make it simple and tell what really happened."

"Biff . . . " She looked at him imploringly.

He looked at her, me, then back at her again, and finally shrugged and said, "Go ahead."

"Friday, when Roddy had the accident," she said. I

nodded, trying to look agreeable, trying to keep her talking. She shook her head. "It wasn't an accident."

"You don't know that for sure," Birnbaum corrected.

"Okay. I don't *know* that. Biff is right."

"Just tell us what you were going to tell us," I said.

"When the big stone fell, I was standing on the other side of the clearing. I happened to look up just as it fell and I saw Jack Scott running away from the ledge." She looked to Birnbaum as if for permission to continue. He nodded again.

"That's why I wanted to talk to him. I had to tell him that I had seen him. So I called his room and had him meet me outside."

"What did he say?"

"He said I was mistaken, that I couldn't have seen him because he wasn't there."

"And?" I said.

"I told him I *hadn't* been mistaken. That I *had* seen him. He got mad at me and said what the hell reason did he have for trying to kill Tony McCue?"

"That's what he said? McCue?"

She nodded. "And I yelled back at him and told him he'd better not be trying to get Biff into any trouble. And then he kind of stomped off."

"And what did you do?"

"I came back and I told Biff about it, and then I was all upset so Biff gave me a couple of sleeping pills and I went to bed. I slept until the morning."

"And what did you do, Biff?" I asked.

He started to answer, then stopped as the door opened and Chico entered.

"You all know my associate, Miss Mangini," I said. "You were saying?"

"I didn't see Jack that night. So I thought I'd talk to him in the morning. And then in the morning, he was dead. So I didn't mention it. Nothing against you, Sheila, but I didn't even know if it really happened."

"It did," Sheila insisted.

"I know that you believe it did. But by the morning, Jack was dead and I didn't think it'd serve any purpose to muddy his name that way."

Chico leaned against the back of the couch and nodded to me.

"Okay," I said.

"What are you going to do?" Birnbaum asked.

"For the time being, I'm going to let sleeping dogs lie," I said.

"I wish you would," Birnbaum said. "This movie is going to fold. Without Jack, the investors are pulling out and I'm just going to close it down. There just isn't any point in making things worse by saying what Jack might have done or tried to do or maybe didn't try to do but somebody thought he did."

"He did," Sheila said.

"I want to talk it over with Chico. Maybe it's not necessary to tell anyone," I said.

"That's what I believe is best," Birnbaum said. "Come on, Sheila. We've got to start making phone calls and heading off everybody before they get here tomorrow." He left the room with Sheila, as usual, trailing behind him.

Chico closed the door behind them and waited until they would be well out of earshot.

"Same down there," she said. "The dumbwaiter door in Birnbaum's room was opened and then sealed again."

She started as a knock sounded on the door behind her ear. It was Clyde Snapp, who handed Chico a piece of paper, grinned at me, and left.

"You do good work, Trace," said Chico after looking at the paper.

"How's that?"

"Tony's digoxin was loaded with potassium chloride."

"Somebody was trying to kill Tony," Ramona said.

"It looks that way."

"Jack Scott," Ramona said. "That's what Sheila just said. She saw him pushing the rock. It was Scott."

"Maybe," Chico said. She showed me the note and it started finally to get a little clearer.

But only a little.

33

Autumn jumps on upstate New York with both feet. It was still early in the evening, but already it was deep dark outside as we sat in the warmly lit dining room. Everyone was there except Pamela Scott. Biff Birnbaum was talking.

Chico had told me he was a cokehead and now I wondered why I hadn't noticed it before. His eyes were shiny, kind of manic-looking, and he almost seemed to vibrate with nervous energy.

"We've finally gotten rid of the people from the press," he said. "I think Tony discouraged them yesterday. Naturally, I don't approve of his language, but I can certainly understand the provocation.

"Anyway, Jack's body has been released to the funeral home and Pamela will be going back to New York City tonight to make arrangements for his funeral.

"And . . . Well, there's no easy way to say this, especially to people I've come to regard as my friends, but we're closing down the film. I've spent the better part of the day talking with the investors and there's too much resistance to going ahead with the project without

Jack. Even if we were to start shooting, I'm afraid we'd run out of money along the way and the project would just go on a shelf somewhere. I don't want you people to have to put in that kind of time and perhaps wind up not getting paid. Sheila and I have tried to contact everybody, but we'll be staying here through tomorrow in case some crew people didn't get our message and show up anyway."

I looked around the room. Tami Fluff looked heart-broken, but that was to be expected, I guess. After all, this was going to be her first straight starring role and now it had been shot out from under her. Arden Harden looked puzzled, and I guessed he was probably trying to figure out what his union contract guaranteed him. He'd be burning up the telephone line to his agent before the hour was up.

Dahlia Codwell seemed to be taking it in stride. She had never liked the idea of playing the star's mother; she might have figured that if she milked a lot of publicity from this disaster, she might be hired up pretty quick for another role.

And then there was Roddy Quine. He was looking around the room, smiling insipidly, and I wondered if he knew at all what was going on.

Tony McCue walked from our table to the bar, turned, and hoisted his glass in a mock salute. "To *Corridors of Death*. Rest in peace." He looked around behind the bar for a moment, then called out to Clyde Snapp, who was standing near the door, "Where's the ice?"

"Sorry. Machine's broken."

Tony shook his head. Then he grabbed an empty glass from the bar and said, "I'm going to get Pamela. She ought to be here with us."

"No," Birnbaum said, but Tony was already going out through the dining room door.

He came back five minutes later with Pamela Scott,

still wearing black. This time his glass was filled with ice, and he went to the bar and splashed gin into it as Pamela Scott stood by his side. Her face was pale; there was a slight discoloration alongside her left eye.

"Is there a drumroll?" McCue said. He looked around. "All right. No drums. Turn down the house lights anyway." He looked toward Clyde, who turned the dimmer switch, and the dining room grew darker.

Tony looked at Mrs. Scott and said, "We're all heartbroken, Pamela, that this weekend has turned out to be such a tragedy. Biff, as you know, is closing down the film and we guess that's the right thing to do. But I know I'm speaking for everyone when I say we had all looked forward to working with your husband and we all thought we could have made a wonderful film here. Of course, the loss of a film is nothing compared to your personal loss, because there will be other days . . . other films. But we all wanted you to know how we felt." He leaned over, kissed Pamela on the cheek, then raised his glass above his head. "To the memory of Jack Scott, America's Boy Next Door."

He sipped his drink, then drained it and, holding the glass in one hand, escorted Pamela to Biff Birnbaum's table.

He seated her and walked back to our table. Just as he pulled out the chair to sit down, he froze in position.

Almost in slow motion, the glass he had drunk from dropped from his hand onto the floor. McCue clapped both hands to his chest. A look of pain wrinkled his face, and suddenly from his lips came a long deep groan, a sound that seemed to come from within a cave.

He doubled over, in obvious pain, then crumpled and fell into a heap on the floor.

Chico screamed. I jumped up and so did Ramona.

"What happened?" a voice called out.

"McCue. He's sick," I yelled.

Ramona knelt alongside him. Her body was over his as expertly she probed into his throat with her fingers, looking for a pulse. She stood up and looked around the dimmed room in total confusion.

"Tony's dead," she said. "He's dead."

Pamela screamed. People looked from one to another as if trying to find someone who would say it wasn't so, that it was all a mistake.

I reached down, picked up McCue's glass, and sniffed it. Most of the liquid and some of the ice had spilled onto the floor.

"This smell funny to you?" I asked Ramona.

She took the glass and smelled it, then touched her tongue to it.

"He's been poisoned," she said. "That's potassium chloride."

"Where'd he get that drink?" I said.

"He made it himself," Harden said. "I saw him."

I turned away for a split second. "But the ice. There wasn't any ice at the bar."

Chico said, "He must have gotten the ice in Mrs. Scott's room." She looked toward Pamela, and as she did, Birnbaum got up and started walking toward the door. I reached out a hand to stop him, but he pushed me away.

"Where are you going?" I said.

"I have to go to the bathroom."

"It can't wait?"

Chico said, "I'm going to Mrs. Scott's room and get the rest of that ice. Mr. Snapp, you'd better call the sheriff. There's been a murder here."

"I've got to go now," Birnbaum said. He pulled away from me and ran toward the dining-room door, but Snapp stepped in his way.

"I don't think anybody ought to leave just now," Clyde said.

Birnbaum stopped short, then turned around. His shoulders dropped.

I heard a scream and turned to see Pamela Scott standing at her table.

"You idiot," she yelled at Birnbaum. "You moronic murderous idiot."

"You two should have gotten rid of the chemicals," I said.

"Jesus Christ. What chemicals?" Harden asked.

"The stuff they were going to use to poison McCue. Before they killed Scott," I said.

"What?"

"You heard me."

Pamela was weeping. Dahlia Codwell stepped over and put an arm around her. Quine was looking back and forth at each speaker as if he were watching the doubles finals at Wimbledon.

There was silence for a moment and into it I said, "They came here planning to poison McCue. And they killed Scott too."

It was silent again except for Pamela, who said softly, "It's true. It's true."

"Don't say a thing," Birnbaum yelled. "This is all nonsense."

"We know it all," Chico said. "You made a mistake with the dumbwaiter rope. It shows you lowered Scott's body from your room."

"You drug-headed jackass," Pamela Scott shouted as Sheriff Len Tillis came into the dining room.

"You heard enough, Sheriff?" I asked.

He nodded. "More than enough."

Pamela wiped her eyes, took a deep breath, and stared across the room at Birnbaum. "Why didn't you get rid of the chemicals?" she said.

"I did," he said.

"But Tony . . ."

She looked at the body on the floor, which slowly uncurled in the dim light, stretched, yawned, and then got to his feet.

Tony McCue was grinning widely. "Tennis anyone?" he called.

"Holy shit," Arden Harden exclaimed. "This is just like a fucking movie."

"Yeah?" Birnbaum said. "Well, it ain't over yet." He moved quickly, diving into Sheriff Tillis, hammering the bigger man to the ground. Before anyone could move toward him, he was on his feet again, with Tillis' revolver in his hand, waving it back and forth at all of us.

"I'm getting out of here," he said. "Nobody better try to follow me. Anybody sticks their head out that door, I'm going to blow it off."

Still holding the gun on us, he backed out through the sliding doors of the dining room, then turned and ran for the hotel's front door.

Tillis lumbered to his feet. "Don't worry, folks. He won't get far. I'll have the roads flooded with troopers in five minutes."

Chico snapped, "Bulldookie." She grabbed her purse and ran for the front door. I followed her and I could feel people coming up behind me.

We got out to the front steps of the building. Birnbaum's gray Cadillac was ripping down the driveway toward the gate of the hotel grounds, open again now that the press had left.

Chico reached into her purse and came out with a long-barreled revolver. She dropped the purse at her feet and, with two hands on the grip, aimed the revolver toward Birnbaum's fleeing car. There was a wild look in her eye, sort of a Charlie's Angel possessed by the devil.

"You're supposed to shout, Freeze," I said.

"Shut up," she snapped.

And then she fired. And then again. And again, squeezing off the shots as rapidly as she could. The driveway lights showed puffs of dirt kicking up around the Cadillac as bullets hit the ground. Chico was grunting as she fired; she sounded like Chris Evert-Lloyd returning a serve.

Then the Cadillac lurched and swerved out of control, just before it reached the gate, and slammed nose-first into one of the stone gate columns.

It rocked back and forth on its springs for a moment, then stopped. Birnbaum did not come out of the car.

Snapp and the sheriff ran by us toward the car. They were each carrying a rifle, which I guess Snapp had stashed somewhere inside the hotel.

As we watched, they ran to the car and Snapp covered them with his rifle as Tillis opened the door, reached inside, and yanked Birnbaum out of the Cadillac. Wearing his silly Mets jacket, he looked small, with Tillis holding him by the neck, like a young kid being collared by the school principal for writing in the halls.

"Hot damn," Chico said.

"Where'd you get that gun?" I asked her. She turned toward me and I said, "Please point it somewhere else. Where'd you get it?"

"I bought it this morning in town. From a friend of Snapp's. While you were sleeping."

"Good shooting," I said.

"Not so good," she said.

"You shot out the damn tire. That's pretty good."

"Yeah, but I was aiming for his head. I wanted to kill the fucker."

"Christ, you are a bloodthirsty thing," I said.

Chico smiled. "And don't you forget it, *kemo sabe*."

34

"All we were worried about was the insurance policy on Tony. But Mrs. Scott had a five-million-dollar policy on her husband. That's what was behind it all."

Chico was talking. The two of us were with Ramona and McCue down in Clyde Snapp's basement kitchen.

"That's why Chico spoke to Walter Marks today," I said. "He's my boss at the insurance company."

"Ex-boss, Trace," Chico corrected. "That's right. There's some kind of clearing house for the insurance industry he was able to check on. There was this giant policy on Jack Scott."

"I don't understand it," Snapp said. "Not even for that kind of money."

"That's why you're you and that's why Birnbaum and Pamela are going to jail,"Chico said. "Look. Here's how it worked. Scott and Birnbaum were in deep trouble. All Birnbaum's pictures had flopped and Scott's television shows were ready to be yanked. That's why they had so much trouble raising money for this picture."

"They even got some money from Bob Swenson, the head guy at the insurance company," I said. "That's why he insisted that I come up here and make sure nothing happened to McCue."

"Now Birnbaum says that it was originally Scott's idea to get the policy on McCue and then kill him and make it look like a heart attack. As you said, Ramona, potassium chloride will do that," Chico said. She went over to look in the walk-in refrigerator. She kept talking.

"What Scott didn't know was that his wife and Birnbaum were lovers. They had been for years, and neither one cared much for him. But he was carrying the ball on poisoning Tony, so they were willing to go along. Scott grew up in Albany; that's where he hired that mob guy to try to kill Tony the first night Trace met him. But the guy just ran over that poor man wearing Tony's hat and coat."

Virtually her whole body vanished into the refrigerator. I said, "Thursday night, when we were out, Scott went up to your room and started to put some chemicals in with your heart medicine. Remember? When you came back, you couldn't get in the door?"

McCue nodded.

"Scott had locked the door from the inside. That's the only way the door can be locked. So he heard you at the door and he knew he was in trouble. He opened the dumbwaiter. Maybe he used a key or something to remove the screw. He heard you leaving the door, so he unlocked it and then scooted into the dumbwaiter shaft. He climbed down to Birnbaum's room, which is right downstairs from yours. He would have pulled it off too, except . . ."

Chico was chewing on a sandwich she had made while leaning inside the refrigerator.

"Except that Trace spotted that the medicine had been tampered with," Chico said. She was chewing on a Dagwood sandwich.

"Scott was furious," she said. "He wanted you dead,

Tony. So the next day he tried to roll that rock over
onto your head. Sheila saw him, but naturally he de-
nied it. When she told Biff about it, Birnbaum was
worried because Scott had been seen. Now if something
happened to McCue, Sheila would implicate Scott and
Scott would implicate Birnbaum and Pamela. Scott was
going to get them all thrown in jail. That was Birnbaum's
worry."

Chico bit off more than she could chew and looked at
me imploringly while she struggled to swallow.

"By this time, though," I said, "they didn't have
access to your room anymore because I had put the
padlock on it. But Scott remembered the dumbwaiter.
And since everybody knew your drinking habits, he
came up with the idea to put the poison in your ice
cubes. He made a tray of cubes in his room with the
chemicals in them. Then he told Pamela to go make
sure Clyde Snapp was occupied. That's when she asked
you, Clyde, to fix the tire; she had just flattened it
herself by letting the air out. I met her in the lobby and
she didn't say a word to me about the tire; then she
went and told you it was flat. See? She wasn't worried
about me. But if Clyde was down here, he might hear
sounds from inside the dumbwaiter shaft. The flat tire
was to get him outside. Then she thought I'd better be
kept away too since my room was next to Tony's.
Harden told me she came upstairs looking for me. I
wasn't there, so she went outside and found me on the
grounds. You know . . . she told the sheriff that she
had taken her shower and gone to bed, but when I saw
her after that, she was still all made up. Women don't
go to bed made up."

Chico had swallowed. "Scott went upstairs to Birnbaum's room with this plastic bowl filled with the poisoned ice cubes. Birnbaum told the sheriff that he tried
then to talk Scott out of it, but Scott wouldn't listen.

He wanted Birnbaum to hoist him up the dumbwaiter shaft to Tony's room, where he could stash the ice cubes in the ice bucket. When you came back and made a drink, bingo. You'd be gone."

She ate some more of the sandwich. I was about to chip in when she started up again.

"Anyway, Scott and Birnbaum argued and then got into a fight. To hear Birnbaum tell it, Scott fell against the side of the dresser and broke his neck, but I don't know if I believe that. The ice cubes were on the shelf by the open dumbwaiter and the whole bowl got knocked down the dumbwaiter shaft. Birnbaum hung the body in the rope and then just used muscle to lower the rope to get the body down below the level of Scott's own room. But if you look at the dumbwaiter rope carefully, you can see how much of it has been pulled through the pulley. It measures sixteen feet, and that's just how far Birnbaum's dumbwaiter door is above the spot where Scott's body was found."

I wanted to say something too, so I blurted out, "The ice cubes that had dropped melted by morning. That's when you, Clyde, saw the water dripping out and found the body and then mopped up the water."

"But the container," Chico said, "and the paper towels you used showed a heavy trace of potassium chloride. And then tonight, when Tony ran his drop-dead scam, Birnbaum thought that Pamela had somehow gotten more of the chemicals into the ice tray in her room. He was on his way to get rid of all of that when we stopped him."

She stopped and shrugged.

"Poor Biff didn't know," I said, "that Chico had already taken Mrs. Scott's ice-cube tray to have the lab analyze it. She put in the one from Tony's refrigerator tray."

"What put you on their trail?" McCue asked Chico. "That's the part I don't understand."

"When I arrived early this morning, the hotel was dark. Everybody was asleep for the night. Except I saw somebody walking around the grounds. Two people. At first, I thought it was Trace out tipping on me . . ."

"Perish forbid," McCue said. "He's the picture of fidelity."

"Well, I saw that it wasn't him, but of course I didn't know anyone here, so I didn't recognize who it was. Today at breakfast, when Birnbaum came in wearing his Mets jacket, I recognized the jacket. And then I recognized Mrs. Scott when she came into the dining room. When I saw them last night, they were obviously more than grieving partner and grieving widow." She looked at Ramona for reinforcement. "You can tell things like that," she said, and Ramona nodded.

"I'll be damned," Clyde Snapp said. "I've got to hand it to the two of you. Pretty darn smart."

"Don't hand it to me," I said. "Hand it to her. I figured if there was a killing, it was the owner of the hotel trying to get publicity to drum up business. That tells you how smart I am."

"I remember you tried that on me yesterday," Snapp said. "I told you it couldn't be."

"Well, I didn't know that," I said. "I don't know the owner of the hotel."

"*I'm* the owner," Snapp said. "I just don't like a lot of people knowing about it, otherwise they start asking me for money. I guess I'm gonna have to try to find a new movie company to come here."

"I think once the press finishes having a field day with the murder," McCue said, "you're going to have to fight off the bookings."

"I sure hope so," Snapp said. "Truth is, I think I had enough of movie folks."

*   *   *

Before we went to bed, Chico said, "I sort of feel sorry for Pamela Scott. Her husband was a wife-beater—that's why she was always wearing sunglasses or that heavy theater makeup—and she didn't have much of a life."

"Murder's still against the law," I said.

"I know that. But first she was pushed around by Scott and then I suspect it was Birnbaum who decided to kill her husband for his own insurance policy. Drugheads get a sense of power like that. I think she was just kind of dragged along."

"That's her problem," I said. "It's a free country and you can walk. But if you hang around, then it's your decision. It's like Sarge says: lie down with dogs, get up with fleas. She was lying down with dogs. Both Scott *and* Birnbaum. Biff sure didn't give a damn about her when he was trying to lam out of here before."

Still later, Chico said to me, "Aren't you happy I came up here?"

"No."

"Why not?"

"Because you're doing like detective crap and I'm not buying," I said. "All I want to do is be left alone."

"Trace, don't knock it. Our firm's going to be famous."

"I don't want to be a famous detective," I said.

"Don't worry. You won't be."

"How's that?" I said.

"You're too dumb to be a famous detective."

It was the nicest thing anybody had said to me in a long time.